Polar Opposites

Amity Allen

Contents

Chapter 1

I'd never been so glad to get off a plane in my life. I thanked the heavens I was still alive as I tumbled across the tarmac toward a figure waiting in the dimness.

When I turned to wave at the jolly-faced pilot in the bush-plane's doorway, my hand shook. Maybe it was nerves from having been on the most harrowing flight of my life in a tiny aircraft that didn't absorb any turbulence. Or perhaps it was the shock to my system from stepping into frigid air when I was used to the California sun. I didn't know, nor did I care to figure it out at that moment. It was enough to be on solid ground, alive.

I continued toward the round figure that waited for me, squinting in an attempt to get a better look. It didn't work. All I could see was a weird pale yellow light around the figure. Where was that coming from? It didn't seem right.

I was forced to wait until I was within a few feet to make out the features of a woman with olive-colored cheeks and long black lashes. That was pretty much all I could see—she was wrapped in a fur coat with the hooded fringe pulled so tightly her mouth and nose weren't visible.

The voice that emerged from the fur made me think this was a woman, and the tiny lines around her eyes suggested she was near my age—somewhere close to thirty. "Hi, you must be Frankie. You're going to need a better parka." She waved a mitten up and down in front of me.

Wracked by a full-body shiver, I glanced at the orange ski jacket I'd read every review on the internet on and paid almost the equivalent of a car payment for before embarking on the journey to Frost Peak, Alaska. "This one is rated for negative thirty degrees." Another shiver slammed home the fact that my protest was in vain. Parka lady was obviously right.

Ignoring my feeble argument, she said, "Your granddad sells parkas, and I can help you pick out which one will work best. I'm Nina Montes, by the way. Your granddad asked me to come collect you. It's nice that you came up here to help him. I'm sorry for the loss of your grandmama."

I swallowed and nodded my thanks. It was still hard to think about her being gone.

I flashed back to the phone conversation with Grandpa a couple months earlier. The one during which he'd told me he was having some trouble running his store. He hadn't said it outright, but I'd gotten the idea his memory was slipping. That broke my heart and sent a thrill of fear through me.

I couldn't leave him alone in the Alaskan wilderness, fumbling to keep his business going.

Of course, I hadn't been able to say yes right away because I was supposed to get married in a month. And Chad would never move to Alaska. Luckily—yeah, let's call it that—he broke up with me that very evening, before I was even able to tell him about Grandpa. I was heartbroken for about half an hour, but then I remembered Chad was condescending more often than I should have ever put up with. I was still sad after that, but more about life plans not going my way. I was in my thirties and not married yet.

And I sure didn't want to jump back into the dating pool where I lived. Can we say *humiliation*?

Putting a couple thousand miles between me and my ex—and our group of friends—suddenly became quite the appealing prospect, and I'd poured myself into getting ready for a new life in the arctic.

That certainty had lasted the whole time I sold things, shipped belongings, and wrapped up loose ends.

It evaporated when I started the journey. Since then, I'd done nothing but second-guess myself. What if I hated my new home? What if I didn't meet my Grandpa's expectations? What if I'd make a horrible mistake? Even—and I shudder to admit I even thought it—should I go back and make up with Chad?

Interrupting my thoughts, Nina swept a hand around us. "Welcome to Frost Peak, where the temperature, the earthquakes, the wildlife, and the townsfolk could each kill you in thirty seconds or less."

I swallowed hard. "Uh. Thanks?"

She chuckled. At least, I thought it was a chuckle. It was hard to tell from within the fur. "I'm joking. It would take at least thirty minutes for the temperature to get ya. Let's go."

I adjusted the straps on my hiking backpack and followed her toward a shack-like building on the edge of the tarmac as the sound of the deathtrap—erm, bush plane—taking off filled the air behind us. Within the noise, there was another lower rumble that didn't seem to come from the same spot.

Scanning the area, I tried to locate the second sound, but the lighting was so dim.

It's three in the afternoon. It looks like twilight.

I'd known I was moving to Frost Peak during the dark season, but somehow, I still hadn't been ready for twenty hours a day of no sun.

Nina must have heard the noise too, because she also scanned the area around us. She stopped and focused on something, and I tried to make out what had caught her attention. Sure enough, there was something different from the rest of the horizon in the far distance. An interruption in the frozen landscape. A shape. "What's that?" I pointed. "A person?"

Nina shook her head and turned her eyes back toward me. "Come on. Let's get you to the shop where you can get warm." She moved faster toward the squat shack. "So, you've managed a store before, huh?"

Why did I get the feeling she was trying to distract me?

"Yeah, I've worked in retail since I was eighteen and been in management for about five years." *And I'm good at it.* Since I wasn't a braggart, I only thought about that part. If there was one thing that didn't worry me about moving up here, it was whether I could manage Grandpa's store efficiently.

I increased my pace, the chill seeping through my coat. I glanced at the shape again. Still there. And now that I thought about it, it was too big at that distance to be a person. "Could it be a wolf over there? Oh, maybe it's a moose? I read up on the wildlife here. Did you know a moose can run thirty-five miles per hour? That speed would get it to us fast if it started stampeding. Can a single moose stampede, or is that terminology just for a herd of something? Wait, what was it you said about the wildlife here being killers?"

Nina pursed her lips for a second, then breathed out. "You read a lot, huh?"

"I like to be prepared. So is it? A moose, I mean."

"Nope. It's a polar bear. But it won't get close to us. Especially if we move along quickly." She skirted around the building, me hot on her heels.

"Polar bear? I don't know how fast they run. I should have thought to find that out."

I stopped short when I saw we were heading for a massive black and silver snowmobile. "We're going on that?"

"Yep. It's the fastest and best way to travel out here. And it isn't far." She slid onto the machine gracefully, then jerked her chin at me. "Jump on."

I glanced at the thing, more than a little nervous. I wasn't exactly the most graceful person in the world. I mean, I could ride a bike, but this thing was a lot faster than that. "Is there a helmet or something?"

Even with the fur pressing in close around Nina's eyes, I could see her roll them. "Hustle your muscles, girlfriend. You're not going to get any warmer standing there being a wimp."

That rankled. I wasn't a wimp. Just cautious. I scooted to the snowmobile and threw a leg up, hollering when I banged my knee.

Nina chuckled. "Not a rider, huh? You gotta do a little hop up."

I tried again, this time clearing the machine and climbing awkwardly up behind her, bumping my chin on her shoulder in the process. Luckily, her parka was thick, and it felt like sinking into a marshmallow.

Nina handed a pair of headphones over her shoulder. "Wear these. We can hear each other through them."

I'd barely gotten them on over my knit hat before the snowmobile roared to life. It matched my orange ski jacket, which I'd thought was a great fashion statement, but now I wondered if it would make us a better target for polar bears. Could they see in color? Did they attack orange things?

My polar bear-related education was woefully inadequate.

The snowmobile jerked forward, and I yelped and grabbed Nina's waist.

I was pretty sure she laughed at me.

Once I was stable enough, I glanced over my shoulder, searching the snowy landscape for the bear. I didn't see it, but I did see a swirling mass of snow heading our way. It quickly enveloped us, and I couldn't see farther than Nina in front of me.

"What's going on?"

"A little wind squall. Nothing to worry about."

"But we can't see. What if you hit something?" The snowmobile's headlight only cut into the snow a few feet.

"I got it." She lifted one hand from the handlebar and did a strange motion with her wrist.

I felt a strange sensation. My ears popped like I was going up in altitude, and my vision swam for a second. When it cleared, the entire area ahead and to both sides of us lit up over a twenty-foot half-moon radius. "What is that? Where's that light coming from?"

Nina's voice came through my headphones. "I did a quick spell."

"Spell? What are you talking about?"

There was silence in response. Nina twisted the snowmobile's throttle, and we shot forward. I yelped and tightened my hold again.

After a few minutes, we were out of the snow squall, and the strange light went out. Nina slowed the machine and said, "I thought you knew. You know, by seeing my aura like I saw yours."

Aura? I thought about the yellow glow I'd seen around Nina. I'd forgotten as soon as I started talking to her. "Knew what?"

"That I'm a witch. Like you."

A witch?

A chill that had nothing to do with my sub-par jacket skittered up and down my spine. I was on a snowmobile in the middle of the tundra with a madwoman. I hadn't even questioned her story that she was sent by my grandfather. Back in the city, I never would have fallen for something like that, but I must have let my guard down because I was in tiny Frost Peak.

My mind raced, trying to figure out how to stay safe.

Nina's voice came through the headset again. "Never mind. Let's get you to your grandfather, okay?"

"Okay. Thanks."

Yeah. Get me to my grandfather.

Nina seemed nice, and I'd thought maybe we could be friends, but it turned out she was crazy, and I'd have to steer clear. If she took me to town at all.

Story of my life.

As we bumped across the expanse of white ground, I tried to see through the snow, looking for the bear. And even though I didn't see it again, I got the strange feeling someone was watching me.

We pulled up in front of Spitzer's General Store, and I was so relieved I could have cried. Nina might be crazy, but she wasn't the brand of crazy that took a city slicker out into the Alaskan wilderness and dropped her off.

Yay.

I turned my attention to the store, blinking a few times to make sure it was real.

I'd been to visit my grandparents in Frost Peak a dozen times or so after Mom and I moved away when I was two. There were some cousins who lived in nearby villages, and I could remember visiting with them. Most of the rest of it was sort of a blur, but each time I was there, I was surprised by the store.

It was huge and beautiful.

I'd thought maybe it was in my memory that way because I was smaller in stature the last time I'd seen it. But nope. My mind's eye hadn't magnified the majesty of the place at all.

Spitzer's was a towering, two-and-a-half story log cabin-style building with a central peak featuring a magnificent arched window in the second story and huge rectangular ones along the place's entire face. Gnarled wood posts held up a vast porch roof, angled metal, so the snow would slide off.

The store's imposing beauty was deepened by the setting—the Brooks mountain range on the north side of Frost Peak created a ruggedly gorgeous backdrop for the store and the town, reminding me we were within the Arctic circle.

Grandpa's store sat on the edge of Frost Peak, between a little post office and a big house. I knew the house was owned by Bob Dearing.

He rented out some of the rooms, making his place more like a hotel. This spot was like a little hub in the tiny town of Frost Peak.

"Let's get you inside before you freeze, Cali-girl." Nina headed up the rough-hewn steps, boots thudding on the wood. How could she be so graceful in all those thick clothes?

As she reached for the door handle, it flew away from her hand, and the door opened.

There stood George Spitzer, my beloved grandfather, looking exactly as he had my whole life—like an emaciated version of Santa, complete with the long white beard, black suspendered pants, and rosy cheeks. He was only missing the round, jiggly belly. He pinned Nina with a sharp-eyed look. "Did you fetch her? Was it a rough flight? Is she traumatized?"

"I didn't do the piloting—Sal did. I met her at the strip." Nina jerked a finger toward where I stood at the bottom of the steps. "She doesn't have a decent coat. And she did look a little traumatized. Sal's flying'll do that to anybody."

Grandpa's gaze landed on me, and he hooked his thumbs in his suspenders and leaned back, smiling broadly. "My girl," he breathed. Then, louder, "Frankie Banks, get your skinny behind up here out of the cold." He disappeared into the store with Nina on his heels.

I shook my head and grinned. Like Grandpa had any business calling anyone else's rear end skinny. If the man turned sideways and hid his beard, he'd be easy to mistake for a pole.

As I started for the steps, I blew out a breath, which froze into a puff of icy air. It was so cold. And so dark. My heart felt joy at seeing Grandpa, but had I leaped into this move too fast? I already missed the California sun.

A feeling like icy water skittered between my shoulder blades and left an itchy feeling. The kind you get when someone's looking at you as you walk away. I spun and scanned the street. There were a few scattered houses which were all squat compared to the general store but decorated in bright colors, as was the custom this far north.

A couple of snowmobiles and one big truck rumbled by a block or so away, but no one looked my direction. Still, I couldn't shake the feeling someone was watching me. I sprinted up the steps, stumbling on the last one.

I was going to have to up my game if I was to be as agile in winter clothes as Nina. Maybe there was some kind of fully-dressed aerobics class people who lived this far north could take to develop the skill. I'd have to ask Grandpa.

Entering the store made me almost instantly forget the cold, dark, and eerie feelings I'd had on the street. The place was bright, airy, organized, and seemingly out of place for the rugged arctic town. Chandeliers hung at intervals, fitted with full-spectrum bulbs that helped fight seasonal affective disorder, and though it wasn't possible, it seemed like they started helping me immediately.

Grandpa was behind a long counter to my right, talking to a young woman whose dark wavy hair reminded me of my own except it was barely past her shoulders, and mine hit my waist. She glanced at me and grinned. It hit me this was Nina, her hood lowered and parka undone at the top. I'd been right—she was around my age. She waved me over, and I went, catching Grandpa in a tight hug.

When we separated, I looked around. "I see this place is the social hub of the town, like it always was."

Most of the people I could see in the store weren't looking at merchandise. They were gathered in small groups, chatting and laughing.

Grandpa nodded. "Folks do like coming in here to hear the latest gossip and talk about what's new."

"Is anyone buying anything?"

"Course." He frowned and added, "Not as much as I'd like."

I caught the undertone of concern in his voice and wrapped an arm around his waist. "We'll fix that up. Don't worry. Maybe we need to get a few new products in here. You know, drum up some excitement."

"Easier said than done," muttered Nina.

I raised my eyebrows.

She shrugged. "As you experienced, the last leg of the journey into Frost Peak is a small bush plane. We do get trucks intermittently too, but in the winter, both are heavily influenced by weather. Sometimes, neither can get through. Supplies can be tricky to keep flowing here."

"Hmm." I didn't doubt what she'd said, but my positive nature struggled to swallow it. There had to be a way to get cool stuff into the store that would get people's attention.

"There's nothing wrong with our product selection," Grandpa snapped. "Long as I remember to order on time, anyway, and Aput helps me with that." He gestured to a dark-haired young man stocking shelves. He was wide at the shoulders and narrow at the hips and didn't look older than nineteen.

Nina leaned toward me. "Aput's family has lived here for generations. He's a good kid. Helps your granddad a lot."

I nodded, grateful Grandpa had someone like that around.

"I'm serious about you getting a new jacket," Nina said. "If you want, I'll tell you which of the ones your granddad carries here I'd recommend."

"Sure. Thanks." I slipped off my jacket, dropped it on a chair, and followed her.

We spent the next half hour talking about coats and boots. I kept an eye on the customers who filtered by, chatting with a few who looked my way. The sooner I could learn who everyone was and gain rapports with them, the better.

As we headed back toward the counter with the items I'd chosen, a man stepped in front of us. "Are you new here?"

I halted and leaned back as he got way inside my personal space bubble.

Nina rolled her eyes, grabbed the stuff from my hands, and continued toward the counter.

I stepped back. "Um, no. Yes. Kind of."

"She's my granddaughter, Lloyd. Come to help me get this place runnin' smoother," Grandpa called.

Lloyd peered at me harder, and I leaned back farther.

The word that came to mind as I tried to stay more than six inches away from the guy was *hawk*. His nose hooked at a nearly ninety-degree angle in the middle of the bridge, and his cheeks were pitted beneath high-set bones. Greasy black hair interrupted by gray streaks brushed his shoulders.

He shoved a piece of paper at me. "Prepper con."

"Pardon me?" Was he speaking a different language? I didn't know much of the Inuit language, but that didn't sound like it. Italian, maybe?

He waved the flyer. "I'm having a prepper con. You should come. If you can't come, you should visit the website at the bottom. You can get quality prepper stuff, straight from a real live prepper. Me."

"Prepper? Oh, you mean like someone preparing for a big disaster?" I took the flyer because it was obvious he wasn't going to stop dangling it next to my nose until I did. It was an amateur job, full of misspelled words and claims of doom and gloom on the way. A frown pulled the corners of my mouth down.

"Disaster?" Lloyd snorted. "More like apocalypse. Whoever isn't properly prepared will be in a perfect pickle."

"Nice alliteration."

"Huh? A liter of what?"

I shook my head and pressed my lips together. Chad hadn't liked it when I talked about stuff I'd read or used what he called high-falutin words. I'd tried to train myself to stop, but it hadn't worked.

Then he dumped me, and I was beginning to realize I shouldn't have tried to change for him in the first place. I liked knowing about things like alliteration.

"Thanks. I'll keep this in mind." I raised the flyer in salute and scooted around Lloyd, who'd spotted his next mark and approached a man and child, waving another flyer at them as he went. I listened in for a minute. My eyes popped wide when I heard him tell the guy he shouldn't buy fishing line at the general store but order it from Lloyd's website instead.

This guy was trying to steal Grandpa's customers right out of the store.

I turned on my heel to follow Lloyd, abandoning my path toward Grandpa and Nina. I edged in so my back was to Lloyd and smiled at the man and his daughter, interrupting the prepper's tirade about aliens taking over the planet any day. "Hi, there. Can I help you find anything?" I glanced at another person in the fishing aisle—a woman with dirty-blonde hair and a large frame. She didn't appear to be paying attention to us at all, which was good. I wanted to handle this with the least amount of disruption to the other customers as possible.

"No, we're fine; thank you. We needed this, that's all." The man gave me a grateful look as he grabbed the fishing line and his daughter's hand and darted around me toward the check-out.

"Hey! You'll be sorry when the aliens come, and you don't have a good enough fishing line to catch a meal!" Lloyd hollered, shaking his flyer.

I forced a smile. "Thanks for the flyers and the information." I used my body movement to herd him toward the door. "I hope the rest of your day is great."

He scowled. "I'm not ready to go. There's more people here for me to talk to." Lloyd reached into his pocket to pull out more flyers, but along with the pages, something else came out and hit the floor.

We both looked down. It was a package of ammunition, with a Spitzer's General Store label plastered on the front.

I frowned and stooped to pick it up. That was when I noticed both his pockets were bulging. "Hey. Did you pay for this stuff?"

His eyes darted in my grandfather's direction, but Grandpa was busy with the guy and his daughter. Lloyd looked back at me and sneered. "You can't prove nothing. I could have brought this stuff in with me."

"You could have, but you didn't. You stole it! Give it to me. All of it."

"I ain't going to. You can't make me. You're a girl and a city-slicker at that. You couldn't make a rattlesnake shake his tail at ya, let alone force a big guy like me to do anything."

His metaphors didn't have to make sense for me to understand what he meant. "You're not big. And I *can* get you to give my grandfather's stuff back." I cut my eyes around and spotted what I needed. I dashed toward the wood-burning stove by the big front window, grabbed a poker from the stand, and brandished it at Lloyd. "Empty your pockets!"

Dimly, I realized there were at least half a dozen people watching the confrontation, maybe more. But I focused on Lloyd, pointing my fire poker at his hook nose.

For a second, I thought he was going to obey me. Then he burst out laughing and headed for the door. "That's a real trouble-maker you got there, George," he called to Grandpa. "Better put a leash on her if you want to keep your business alive."

He slammed out the door. Fury made the edges of my vision darken, and I started after him.

"Frankie!" Grandpa's sharp tone stopped me in my tracks. "Let him go."

I leveled a shocked look at him. "But he stole a bunch of stuff."

Grandpa crooked a finger at me. With a huff, I trudged over to the counter. In a low voice, he said, "Lloyd Dawes is a character. You'll find your fair share of 'em here in Frost Peak. Best you learn to pick your battles."

I couldn't believe my ears. He was fine with that guy taking stuff? Costing the store money? Well, I wasn't. "Shouldn't we at least call the police?"

He and Nina erupted into laughter.

"What's funny?"

"We don't have police," Nina said. "We have a sheriff. One guy. Name's Jason Brodie." She wrinkled her nose. "He's not worth calling."

Grandpa shook his head. "Now, now, Nina. Don't be letting your personal history with the sheriff affect your respect for the position."

She crossed her arms. "I'm not. It isn't the poor guy's fault I was too much for him." She winked.

"We could call the sheriff, but it would take a while for him to get to it. He might arrest Lloyd, but he'd be in the jail in town for a week, at the most." Grandpa gave me a kind smile. "Things are different here, honey."

"So different that people can shoplift with no consequences?"

Grandpa's tone turned sad. "Lloyd's not well. He truly thinks something crazy is going to happen soon and that he needs to be ready."

I leaned on the counter, calming down a bit; though I still found it outrageous that nothing could be done about a proven shoplifter. "He's negative," I grumbled. "Scares people, I bet. He should lighten up. See the glass as half-full."

Grandpa chuckled and shook his head. "I'm glad you're here, honey. Let me show you around."

I spent the next couple of hours getting the lay of the land at the store. Grandpa showed me around the shop, including the back room where inventory was kept. He introduced me to Aput, and I learned his name meant Snow in the Inuit language. He had a shy smile and easy-going mannerisms. I liked him right away, even without already knowing what a help he was to my grandfather.

Grandpa showed me how to work the cash register, which was easy, and I even waited on some customers. A few times, he suggested I head upstairs to the flat I was going to share with him and rest, but I was too amped up for that. At some point, I'd crash, no doubt, but for now, I was too involved in learning the ropes.

After all, helping Grandpa straighten things out with the store had been the reason I came.

It didn't take long for me to notice it—Grandpa's memory definitely wasn't what it used to be. He told me a couple of things more than once. Got confused about when delivery day was and frustrated himself. Told me the wrong code to get into the inventory software and then couldn't remember the real one.

Aput followed Grandpa around, gently helping him without being overt about it, and I kind of loved him for it.

For all the worrying I'd done on the journey, it was clear I'd made the right decision. Grandpa needed me.

There was a steady stream of customers after six pm, and I got into a groove of waiting on folks. When I finally looked up from the cash register and found no one in line to be checked out, it was past seven and closing time.

I glanced around but didn't see Grandpa or Aput anywhere. I busied myself counting down the drawer—that was something I knew how to do without being taught, thanks to years of working in retail. Then I found the vacuum in a closet behind the counter and got to work cleaning up the store. At some point, Aput showed up, and he took the vacuum from me and began working wordlessly. Then Grandpa appeared from the back room. "Time to knock off, kiddo," he said with a grin. "I was thinking we could go to Charlie's for dinner tonight, since it's a special occasion."

"What's Charlie's, and what's the special occasion?" I wondered.

"Charlie's is a diner down the street," Aput interjected. "They have excellent fish and chips."

"You'll come with us, of course, Aput. And, my dear Frankie, of course the occasion is that my granddaughter has come to be with me. You can't know how much it means that you're here." He held out his hands and squeezed mine when I put them in his bigger, more callused ones.

I smiled into his face. "I'm so happy to be here. Thanks for including me." Even though Grandpa knew his memory wasn't the best and that was why I was there, I didn't want him believing it was the only reason. And it wasn't. I needed a change. Wanted one.

When I first arrived, the gruffness of the terrain and the reality of perpetual darkness had jolted me, made me wonder if I had totally messed up by coming to Frost Peak. But as I looked into my grandfather's kind face, I felt settled about it. This was going to be good.

"I'd love to go to Charlie's with you guys. I'm going to take out the garbage real fast. The dumpster's in the back, right?"

Grandpa nodded. "It's down the brick pathway a little ways. I didn't want it too close to the building in case it got stinky. Aput keeps the walkway nice and shoveled and ice-free for us back there."

"Thanks, Aput." I grabbed the big black trash bag and headed for the back door. Before I went out, I remembered to pull on my new parka. Grandpa had insisted its cost was part of my pay for the month, and I hadn't argued much. The jacket I'd been wearing when I arrived was clearly subpar for living in the tundra, no matter what its internet reviews had said.

Grandpa and Nina had also made sure I had a nice pair of fur-lined mittens that were rated for fifty below zero, and I put those on too before I went out. I tried to grab the trash bag and fumbled for a couple of minutes, wondering how people up here managed to do daily tasks like this wrapped in so many clothes. It was going to take some practice, that was for sure.

Finally, I managed to get the trash bag well in hand and headed out the back door. As I stepped onto the brick pathway Grandpa had told me about, I noticed all the stars in the sky. There wasn't much light pollution in the far north, and the night sky made that obvious.

It was breathtaking.

I shook myself. I couldn't stand there gawking forever. Grandpa and Aput must be hungry, and they'd wanted to get to Charlie's right away. I started walking and promptly pitched forward when my foot came into contact with something I hadn't seen on the pathway. By some miracle, I managed to right myself without smashing my nose into the walkway, and once I wasn't teetering anymore, I whirled around to see what had tripped me.

I was expecting to see a piece of wood dropped from someone's arms when they were carrying it in to replenish the woodstove or perhaps a decorative rock or a loose brick from the pathway. So it took my mind a few seconds to register what I was actually seeing.

I gasped, my free hand automatically going to my mouth, which only had the effect of me smacking myself in the face with a heavy mitten. I dropped the trash bag and knelt down to convince myself I wasn't seeing things. Nope. It was someone's boot, still attached to a foot and leg.

Insanely, the kids' song about connected bones skittered through my mind.

As I continued to move my gaze up, I saw the whole body, mostly off the path. I scooted forward to roll the person over and gasped in a draft of frigid air.

It was Lloyd Dawes.

And if I had to judge by the blood-soaked, caved in left side of his skull, I'd have to say he was dead.

Chapter 2

"So you had to bring a little bit of that California drama here with you, huh?" Nina leaned against the counter and gave me an amused look.

"It had nothing to do with me. Just bad timing, I guess." I'd spent the morning trying to forget about what had happened the evening before, but Nina had arrived at the store and was making it very hard for me to do so. She got right in my face almost immediately, wanting to know all the details about how I'd found Lloyd, what happened to him, and all the drama that had ensued after I ran into the shop and screamed, "Someone's been murdered outside!"

And, boy, had there been drama. It seemed like everybody and their brother showed up—everyone except the town sheriff. Some medical staff arrived first, then most of the town's population, and then Frost Peak's only funeral director had pulled up in an old, beat up Buick station wagon with spikes on its tires. He'd rubbed his neck and surveyed the situation, then commandeered a few of the brawny local guys standing around to put Lloyd's body in the car. He'd sped off, but a bunch of townspeople remained, all gossiping and coming up with crazier and crazier stories about what could have possibly happened to Lloyd.

We'd never made it to Charlie's. Instead, Grandpa and I made some sandwiches in the apartment upstairs and fell into bed once we finally got everyone out of the shop around ten pm.

"I don't believe in bad timing." Nina drummed her fingers on the countertop and looked thoughtful. "Do you think it had something to do with that argument the two of you got into?"

"You mean the argument about how he should return the stuff he stole from my grandfather? Why would it have anything to do with that?"

"I don't know. It seems so coincidental, that's all. But Lloyd didn't get along with a lot of people around here, so it probably is only a coincidence."

I grabbed a cloth and started cleaning off the counter, wanting to accomplish something while I stood around gossiping. "Why is that? I mean, I know the guy struck me as a bit of a negative ninny. Plus, I don't have any patience for thieves. But why did he have trouble getting along with others around here?"

Nina ran a hand through her wavy hair, stopping to work out a snarl her fingertips encountered. "All kinds of reasons. Lloyd was a real troublemaker. Always rubbing someone the wrong way or actually doing them harm. Like how he was stealing from your grandpa yesterday. That kind of thing was so Lloyd. I've heard talk that he didn't get along with his neighbor or his landlord."

I chewed that over for a second. "Do you think he truly believed the end was coming? Or was that some kind of ruse to squeeze money out of people?"

"I think he believed it. But he *also* tried to use it to squeeze money out of people." Nina chuckled. "We actually have a pretty active prepper community in Frost Peak, but I don't think he was especially welcome there either. My ex-boyfriend, Phil Albertson, is the leader of that group. He always tried to avoid Lloyd—said he was belligerent and not helpful at all."

"You dated a prepper?" I didn't know Nina very well, but I got the idea she was way too down-to-earth to deal with that kind of negativity.

She waved a hand. "Yeah, not for very long. Anyway, Phil did everything he could to keep Lloyd from knowing when the meetings were. Somehow, the guy always figured it out, though." She dissolved into giggles. "You should've seen Phil's face when Lloyd crashed their annual award banquet. Phil was fit to be tied."

"Preppers have award banquets?" This conversation was opening up a whole new world I had known nothing about.

"Oh, yeah. They have fundraisers, retreats, bunker-building parties—anything you can think of that other groups do. I always thought they were more of a social club than anything. They could've been a knitting group if they weren't preppers. Not that I'm trying to diss preppers or anything. Alaska's full of them. And you do have to prepare for natural disasters around here. I mean, we're always having a blizzard or an earthquake or something, and you never know when one of those will knock out electricity for a few weeks. So really, everyone up here is a prepper to some degree. They don't all believe the end is going to come because of aliens, though. Anyway, like I said, the list of suspects who had motive to kill Lloyd is probably about as long as my arm."

How interesting.

But I was ready for a change of subject. In between worrying about what had happened to Dawes during my sleepless night, I'd also spent a fair amount of time thinking about what Nina had said about spells and auras and recognizing each other as witches. I wanted to ask her more about that.

But another voice interrupted before I could. "Since when are you on the payroll at the sheriff's department, Nina Montes?"

We both swiveled toward the man approaching, whose appearance was as gruff as the tone of voice he'd used. His parka had a leather outer shell with a star-shaped badge on the left lapel and his last name, Brodie, on the other.

"I haven't yet, but maybe you *should* hire me. Heaven knows you have trouble keeping up with everything on your own around here. *Sheriff.*" She emphasized the word a bit, though not quite enough to be considered disrespectful.

He didn't answer; instead, he turned his attention to me. "I'm Jason Brodie, the sheriff in Frost Peak."

The guy sported the classic male good looks you would expect to find in guys in an old Western movie. He had wide, strong cheekbones and a square jaw covered with at least a few days' growth of beard, not well-trimmed at the edges. More like he'd simply not shaved than that he'd carefully tried to look like he hadn't shaved. A flop of chestnut hair stuck out from under the knit cap he wore.

Brodie was handsome. Enough to make my stomach flop around.

"I'm Frankie Banks. George Spitzer's granddaughter. Good friends call me for Frankie Banksy, but I don't have any close enough friends around here yet to call me that."

He raised one eyebrow in amusement. "George told me you were coming when I stopped in last week for supplies. He was excited about it. It's a nice thing you did, coming to help him out. We all love your grandfather around here."

"If you're trying to win the right to call me Frankie Banksy, complimenting my grandfather will go a long way toward helping you achieve it." I smiled.

"I'm not here to earn the right to call you anything, Ms. Banks. I'm here to ask about the confrontation you had with Lloyd Dawes yesterday before he was killed." He pulled out a pocket-sized notebook and a pen and set them on the counter.

"You already know about that, huh?" Nina leaned on the counter, looking relaxed. "Where were you yesterday when we needed someone to investigate the scene of the crime?"

Brodie cut his eyes toward her. "I was in Altimont, taking care of some police business. And I looked at the scene of the crime this morning. Hey, shouldn't you be at the airport or something? I thought you were studying to be a pilot. Seems like you should be there trying to soak up all the information you can rather than hanging around here being a nuisance during a crime investigation."

She lowered her lids halfway, which made her look like a lazy cat. "Hey, I was here yesterday when Frankie and Lloyd had their argument. Shouldn't you be talking to me too?"

"If I decide to talk to you, I can find you, I'm sure. But right now, I'm here to talk to Ms. Banks. So do me a favor and scram."

Nina grinned. "Fine. But if you do come looking for me, make sure it's only to ask questions about the crime. Don't forget our relationship is over."

I'd almost forgotten Grandpa said these two had dated.

Brodie rolled his eyes. "The way I remember it, I was the one who ended that particular relationship, so I don't think you have anything to worry about as far as me trying to rekindle it. Now, at the risk of repeating myself, *scram*."

She gave him a flirty smile, then winked at me before sauntering away, her hips swaying a little more than necessary.

I couldn't stifle a laugh at her bratty behavior.

Brodie blew out an exasperated breath as he also watched her leave, then returned his attention to me. "So what did you and Dawes fight about yesterday?"

"The fact that he stuffed his pockets with stolen goods from my grandfather's store. Call me crazy, but I thought he should return it all. He disagreed."

Brodie scribbled in his notebook. "I see. So you took it upon yourself to brandish a weapon at him. A fire poker, right? And soon after that, Dawes was dead."

That made my hackles raise. Which was a metaphor I didn't think I'd truly experienced until that moment. But it had never been suggested that I'd murdered someone before, which was what this guy seemed to be doing. "Maybe if you would have been available to arrest him for theft, which is your job, the situation wouldn't have escalated."

His gaze snapped up from the notebook to my face, and I quickly realized my mistake. The way I had worded that sounded as though I were confessing to the man's murder. How could I fix this? I opened my mouth, mind whirring. "I didn't kill Dawes. I only mean that if you'd arrested him like you should have, he would be in jail instead of dead. Because whoever killed him couldn't have then. Not me. Because I didn't kill him." *Shut up, Frankie. You're making it worse.*

He leveled a look devoid of emotion at me. "You're the one who found him, right?"

"Yes."

"How did you know to go looking for him behind the store?"

Was this guy for real? "I didn't go looking for him. I went looking to throw the day's trash in the dumpster." I was uncomfortable with the line of questioning. Seemed like Brodie thought I'd killed Dawes.

My gaze bounced past him as I tried to calculate whether the nearby customers could hear him. It wasn't hard to see they could. Oh, they were trying not to look like they were eavesdropping, but one guy was reading the back of a package of hand warmers upside down.

I refocused on the sheriff. "Are you accusing me of something?"

He smiled slowly, and my traitor of a pulse lurched upward at how cute he was. I was finding this guy condescending, and after Chad, I never wanted to find someone with that personality trait attractive again. My pulse didn't care. It only cared about his adorable smile.

The sheriff said, "If I were accusing you of something, Ms. Banks, you'd know it." He stuffed the notebook in his jacket's inner lapel pocket. "I may have more questions as the investigation continues. Don't leave town." He strode away without so much as a *have a nice day.*

"Don't leave town?" I muttered, glaring at his back. "Why would I leave town? I'm not guilty of anything."

"Don't mind him, honey." Grandpa's voice behind me made me jump. "He's just doin' his job."

I glanced at my grandfather and frowned. "If he were doing his job, he would have been around yesterday to arrest Lloyd. Now he's here making thinly veiled accusations, and I don't appreciate it. I can't believe this is the type of law enforcement Frost Peak has."

Grandpa chuckled. I also couldn't believe he was so nonchalant about the whole thing. "Brodie's all right. He'll figure things out. Give him time."

"Time. How much time will it take him while he's gallivanting around taking care of other towns too? Long enough for the killer to get away?"

Grandpa patted my hand and wandered off.

I puffed out a breath. Between the unsettling conversation with Brodie, my upset over the fact that I'd found a murder victim in the first place, and the strange feelings I had about Nina's mention of magic, I was pretty grumpy.

I decided to pull out the mop while I considered everything rolling through my mind. By the time the floor behind the cash register was sparkling clean, I'd figured something out. At the moment, I could only do anything about one of the items I had on my mind. And I planned to get to doing it right away.

Chapter 3

Grandpa had Nina's number, so I texted and asked her to come to the store when she had time. She texted back right away that she'd be there around closing time. That suited me—I didn't want to have this conversation while a bunch of customers were in the shop.

I'd already made the mistake of arguing with Lloyd in front of customers.

Luckily, the shop had a busy spell, and I was able to put other thoughts aside to focus on my work. I was lost when it came to helping folks pick out equipment, so I made sure to listen in on Grandpa and Aput doing it whenever possible.

After the place was cleaned up and the drawer counted, Aput headed out with a wave to me. He held the door open, and Nina breezed in, shoving back her parka hood. "Hey! I'm here. What'd you want to talk about?"

I locked the door behind Aput. "I was hoping to ask you some questions about what you said when we were on the snowmobile yesterday."

"I thought we already found you a proper coat." She pulled her parka off, tossed it on the counter, and leaned on an elbow.

"Not that. The thing about a spell and my aura. Specifically, the thing where you said we're witches."

Nina arched a brow. "What about it?"

"Was that some kind of Alaskan figure of speech I don't understand?"

Slowly, she shook her head.

"I didn't think so." I'd been sure Nina was off her rocker when she brought up the thing about spells. But since then, she hadn't shown any indication of being completely crazy. In fact, I'd found her to have a good head on her shoulders after Lloyd was killed.

She'd come right out when I called and then got to work keeping people away from the scene, even though there were already so many footprints in the snow around the area that they'd never help anyone figure out what had happened. Still, Nina had been steady, and it had made me reconsider my judgment of her. "You're saying you can actually do magic?"

She opened her mouth to answer, but behind her, Grandpa descended the steps from our flat, and I made a cutthroat motion to get her to stop.

Nina glanced over her shoulder. "You don't want to talk about magic where he can hear?"

I widened my eyes and tried to telepathically tell her to shut it. She only laughed. "Cali-girl. Come on. Don't tell me you can't see his aura."

Grandpa stopped at the bottom of the steps and tipped his head. "I bet she's pushed it out of her mind."

"Huh. Why would she do that?"

He shrugged. "That's what humans do when they come across something their brain can't make sense of. They sort of... don't let themselves notice it."

"Can you guys please talk to me like I'm in the room?"

They both turned toward me. Grandpa said, "Kiddo, whatever Nina told you about magic is true. She's a witch. So am I. A lot of folks in Frost Peak are."

"All but a few," Nina added.

I leaned on the counter, trying to be casual but needing the support to stay steady. "Okay." I drew out the word, trying to get my brain to catch up. "And witches should recognize each other because of auras?"

Nina nodded.

Grandpa held his arms wide. "I'm guessing you've trained your brain not to see mine."

And just like that, his words triggered something. A memory of being a kid and always seeing my grandfather with a bright white light around him. Grandma had one too—soft blue. At some point, I'd stopped seeing it, and I'd forgot. Until I saw Nina at the airport, I couldn't remember seeing one in a long time.

Now, as he stood before me, I saw the white light again. It burst into existence in an instant, as though it had been waiting for me to notice it. It was a beautiful, bright-white outline around my grandfather.

I gasped and gripped the counter harder.

Before I could force any words out, a fluff of fur shot down the stairs and over to Grandpa, startling me.

"Do we have a cat?" I was allergic to some of them, but I hadn't noticed any symptoms since I'd been there.

"Not a cat." Grandpa scooped up the white creature, holding it aloft for me to see. "This is Timber, my arctic fox familiar."

"Familiar?" The word was choked, and my brain felt addled. As though it struggled to keep up with the information, or maybe was working on shutting off the strange aura input again.

I straightened, pushing away from the counter and telling myself I didn't need it for strength.

I rounded the counter and got closer to peer at Timber. He was absolutely the cutest thing, no bigger than about ten pounds, with pure white fur, a black nose, and sharp, dark eyes.

"Yep. I'm a warlock. With a familiar." Grandpa whispered something I couldn't quite make out and wiggled the fingers of his right hand. My ears popped, and I felt a little woozy. All the lights went out in the store.

I held my breath, not trusting myself to say anything in that moment. This was real. He had done something... supernatural? Paranormal? What was the right word for a situation in which your grandfather made something happen that was completely against all the laws of nature you'd ever learned? I pushed away the question, recognizing it as my mind's attempt to make sense of the weird happening.

Grandpa whispered and flicked again, and the lights came on. He beamed at me and lowered Timber to the ground. The fox sat primly and eyed me with curiosity.

I blew out a breath and slumped onto a log bench that customers used to try on boots. Grandpa sat beside me and squeezed my knee but didn't say anything.

"She didn't know, huh?" Nina said from her spot by the counter.

"I didn't know," I confirmed. "And you're saying I can do this stuff too? Make the light like Nina did in the snowstorm or turn overhead lights on and off?"

Grandpa nodded. "With some instruction, you can. That and a lot more." He glanced at Nina. "I wasn't planning on introducing so soon."

"Then maybe you should have mentioned she didn't know about magic to me *before* I picked her up at the airport, Mr. Spitzer." Her tone was mild and matched the warm smile on her face.

I twirled a finger in my hair, then stopped when I realized I was doing it. It was a nervous habit I'd developed as a child and worked hard to stop in my twenties. "Okay, this is... well, it's weird. I've never met a witch before." I shot a look at Grandpa. "Or I didn't know I had." A thought hit me like a blow to the head. "Wait, was Mom..." I knew the answer before he gave it. Because I'd just then remembered the pale-pink light I'd seen around her when I was a small child.

Grandpa nodded. "She was a witch too, yes. In fact, she's the reason you didn't know anything about it. She wanted you to have an uncomplicated life, even though I told her that wasn't possible for everyone. She disagreed, and it was her decision as your mom. She worried about how hard it would be for you to be different from the other kids. She had a hard time as a child because of her abilities, so she did what she could to block yours, with a spell. It stopped you from automatically learning magic as a toddler."

"Abilities." The word jarred something in me. I thought about how I seemed to have a knack for finding lost items. To the extent that friends were almost constantly asking me over to help them hunt for things. I sometimes knew what would happen before it did. It was never big stuff, and I'd always chalked it up to intuition. Like, I'd sometimes reach to catch something before it even started to fall or avoid a particular route to work, only to hear later there was an accident.

I'd thought it happened to everyone.

My spine straightened. "My wishes." I hadn't thought about it in a long time, but when I was a kid, I'd sometimes make wishes that came true. Things like wishing a scary thunderstorm would stop, only to have it trickle into a light rain almost immediately. Or the time I wished for a dog, and a stray showed up and lay down right outside my bedroom window. There were more, but somewhere along the way, I'd grown up and stopped making wishes. I raised my eyes to meet my grandfather's. "That was magic, wasn't it?"

He nodded. "At least some of it, yes. Your mother couldn't block it entirely."

It was too much to think about at once. Memories shot into my mind, one after the other like staccato beats on a drum. I rubbed my temples. Grandpa's arm curved around me, and he squeezed me to his side.

I felt Nina sit by my other side. "Overwhelmed?"

I peeked at her smiling face. "That's a good word."

"Suck it up, Cali-girl. You're a witch. It's not as cool as being Mexican, like me, but it's pretty rad. You're part of about two percent of the world's population who have paranormal abilities. I mean, I totally made up that statistic, actually, but I think it's about right, based on my own experiences. Frost Peak has more witches, though, like I said. That's why I'm here. I like being around others who practice magic."

She smirked. "That and I read an article that said Alaska has more men than women, and I thought I could have my pick. I started out in Anchorage, but the dating life there wasn't what I'd hoped, so I decided *what the heck?* Let's go farther north and pursue my dream of being a pilot. Hopefully with some gorgeous, rugged, backwoodsy guys around for good measure."

I couldn't help but laugh, and something released in my chest. I took a deep breath. "Okay. I'm a witch, I guess. So what do I do now?"

"I suggest you buy a pointy hat and a long black dress with fringe. I left mine at home, but they're must-have fashion items for a witch about town." Nina kept a straight face for about five seconds before she dissolved into giggles, doubling over.

Timber wandered over to lick Nina's hands, and she ruffled his ears.

"You're hilarious," I said. "And oh, so helpful." I nudged her with my elbow to let her know I was teasing. She actually *was* being helpful and kind in a moment which seemed like a turning point in my life.

Grandpa chuckled and gave me one last squeeze before releasing me. "How about you try something?"

"Something magical, you mean?" He nodded. "Oh, I don't know if I'm ready—"

"No time like the present!" Nina cried, jumping up and causing Timber to hop backward on two legs to avoid getting trampled. She clapped her hands and resembled a schoolteacher, excited to impart some wisdom on a class of wild second-graders. "You don't absolutely have to make up a rhyme to cast a spell, but a lot of spells will work better if you do."

"A rhyme?" I'd always been better at drawing than writing. "I don't know—"

Nina waved off my attempt at a protest. "It's not hard. You don't have to be Hemingway or whatever. Think of something that fits what you want. Like, once I made my friend's bully back off by saying, *You're a meanie, go back to Queensie.*"

I gave her a blank stare, matched by the one Grandpa directed at her.

Nina stammered, "'Cuz he was from Queens. New York."

"Did he?"

She looked baffled. "Did he what?"

"Go back to New York?"

She chuckled. "No, his dad actually got a job in England like two days later, and a week after that, they were gone. He went to the queen, get it?" She didn't wait for a reply, which was good because I couldn't come up with one. "So, anyway, I wanted him to go away, so I basically made up a rhyme that reflected that. Then you put a little oomph into it." She waved her wrist in demonstration, apparently, of the aforementioned oomph.

"I have no idea what you mean."

"She means direct some magic into the spell. So you say some words and sort of point at what you want to affect. Then you will it to happen." Grandpa shrugged. "It's more of an art than a science. You have to just do it. Then practice a lot."

"Point at it, huh? What about all this?" I twisted my wrist like I'd seen both of them do.

Nina shrugged. "That's flair. Flourish, you know? You don't absolutely need it, but it makes you look extra cool."

I blinked three times, not sure if she was pulling my leg or not. When she didn't dissolve into giggles, I determined she meant it. "Okay. An optional rhyme, a point, some intention, and a bit of optional flourish. Got it." I didn't have it. I was so far from having it, I might as well be in a different state from it.

"Great. Let's try something easy." Nina went to a shelf and touched a box of boots. "Move this up and out, then lower it to the floor."

I chewed my lip. "That sounds complicated for a first-timer."

She shook her head. "Nothing you can't handle. Look, I'll do it first." She whispered under her breath—why didn't they ever do their rhymes so I could hear?—and did her little wrist thing. The box floated out of its spot, hovered gently for an instant, and then descended gracefully to the floor. Nina grinned. "See? Easy peasy." She scooped up the box, put it back, and stepped away. "Now you."

I took a deep breath and wracked my brain for what to say. I decided to whisper it, more because I didn't want to be embarrassed by my poetry writing skills. "Big heavy work boots, I'm giving you the scoot scoots," I mumbled under my breath as I pointed at the box, wiggled my wrist around, and tried to broadcast my intention for the box to move.

All three of us—well, four because Timber did it too—stared intently at the box.

It wobbled.

Nina whooped, and Grandpa had a wide grin. I raised my eyebrows. "Did I make that box wobble?"

"It wasn't the wind. This place is airtight," Grandpa said, puffing out his chest, whether with pride over my baby witch accomplishment or the excellent construction of his general store, I couldn't tell.

"Of course it was you," Nina said. "Do it again."

I repeated the whole song and dance, and this time, the box shot out of its spot and straight toward my face. I yelped and hit the floor, barely missing squishing Timber into a pancake. The boots hit the opposite wall and crashed to the floor.

"You did it!" Nina cried, offering me a hand up.

"Sorry," I muttered to the magical arctic fox, who gave me a dirty look.

I picked up the boots, and as I straightened with them in my hands, excitement coursed through me. I'd performed magic. I'd also nearly taken off my own head and barely avoided killing a sweet woodland creature, but I'd performed real magic.

I was a witch. I bit my bottom lip and vowed to try to do good with my gift. Help people. Make the world better.

"Congratulations, honey." Grandpa's tone was low. "Sorry you had to wait so long to have some fun with your abilities."

"Yeah, but you shouldn't do it alone for now," Nina cautioned. "Magic can be finicky, and it takes a lot of practice. We'll have more lessons until you can control the results better."

"Thanks." I returned the boots to the shelf and turned back toward them. "I won't do anything alone." Then I held out my arms and threw back my head. "All hail Broomhilda!" I cried and then laughed and laughed as my new friend and my grandfather hugged me and laughed too.

Chapter 4

The next morning, it took me a few minutes to remember I was a witch. I bounced out of bed, eager to try something with my newfound power. But Nina's warning echoed in my mind, and I grudgingly resisted. Instead, I decided to head out behind the store and clean up the walkway where I'd found Lloyd Dawes' body.

Aput had planned to do it the day before, once Sheriff Brodie said we could, but we'd had a run on customers, and then Grandpa had told him to go on home and leave it for when it was lighter out. Aput did so much around the place. If I could save him one horrible job, I wanted to.

So I grabbed a quick breakfast with coffee, then bundled up and headed downstairs. It wasn't time to open the store yet, and Grandpa was in the shower. I headed out back and surveyed the dirty walkway, ignoring my stomach's strong lurch when I thought about what the stain was.

How was I going to clean this up? I looked around for a hose, but the spigot attached to the wall where one could hook up was empty. Of course. It was too cold to leave a hose out at this time of year.

I got a spray bottle of cleaner from inside. I sprayed the ugly stain on the walkway, but it froze over almost immediately.

Fantastic. Now I had frozen blood rivulets to figure out what to do with.

Then something occurred to me. I could magic this mess away. I considered what rhyme I could use, but Nina's warning popped into my mind. She said I shouldn't try magic alone.

I glanced around and saw a chisel. Aput used it to break up ice patches on the walkway before shoveling. Maybe I should break this up and then shovel away the pieces. I started toward it, but then a rhyme popped into my mind, fully formed. I hesitated, weighing the pros and cons.

Oh, what the heck? I was a witch. If I couldn't use magic to make a despicable task easier, what was the point?

I lifted a hand and said, "Blood in the ice, flow away so nice," before giving it some flourish from my wrist and a push of my will.

Joy surged when the mess at my feet started moving. It was working! I'd made something happen with magic, all by myself.

The feeling lasted only a few moments before I realized it wasn't going the way I'd planned. Instead of simply vanishing or flowing away into the underbrush, the mess at my feet grew and expanded. In the space of thirty seconds, a wide, creaking river of blood-red ice rose on the walk ahead of me. I gulped as my mind raced. What was I going to do about this? I hadn't learned how to do a counter-spell or whatever.

Probably why Nina had said not to do magic alone, huh?

I didn't have time to berate myself right then, so I'd have to put it aside for later. I focused on thinking of a different rhyme. Something else to do. The ice river rose until it was over my head, more like a glacier now. And then, with a terrifying crash, it reversed direction and came toward me. And the store.

"No! No, no, no, no, no," I cried, raising my hands in a feeble attempt to stop the behemoth from crashing into my grandfather's building. Instead, I tapped my head. "Think, Frankie. Come up with a rhyme. Right now!"

Of course, my mind was completely devoid of useful words. But I had to do something. I raised a shaking hand and said, "Glacier of blood, don't hurt this hood."

Hood? Where had that word come from? It didn't even rhyme with blood.

The glacier paused, and I held my breath. Maybe I'd managed to stop it.

Then it creaked, and my eyes widened as it grew even taller and wider. I couldn't see anything before me except the red glacier. My heart pounded faster than ever before in my life. My stomach plummeted toward my feet, and I realized I needed to shift my focus from trying to stop the ice to getting my grandfather out of the building. Aput too, if he'd arrived.

I spun around and took two steps before a nearly deafening sound made my ears ring. A white blur to my right accompanied a second roar and made me dive left and clap my hands to my ears.

I peeked at the shape before me and my heart, galloping so fast a moment before, felt like it had stopped. Before me stood a polar bear, towering three or four feet over my head on its hind legs. It faced the ice glacier, snarling and snapping at the air. It didn't seem to see me.

My heart started back up again, impossibly going even faster than before. It felt in danger of exploding. I scrabbled backward, kneeling to search for a rock or chunk of ice or anything I could hurl at the polar bear to keep him away.

The bear roared again and then made a series of sounds that reminded me of a cross between a person coughing and a dog alternating yipping and barking.

The glacier stopped. With a whoosh, it drew into itself like a reverse tsunami. I watched, wide-eyed, frozen in a crouch.

The ice melted, and it reminded me of water going down a drain. Except it went into an invisible void or something instead and snapped out of existence.

Where there had been so much noise a moment before, only silence was left.

I panted in relief that Spitzer's General Store wouldn't be bowled over by my huge magic mistake.

Then I remembered a massive, terrifying polar bear still stood before me. My eyes felt ready to bug out of my head as I turned them upward to observe the bear.

It dropped to all fours, and, like we were on a teeter totter, I shot to a standing position, prepared to run for my life.

Then he sat on his rear end, looking for all the world like an adorable stuffed animal. A ginormous one that had roared so loudly the space-time continuum might have been split apart and then fought a magical glacier and won.

I held up a hand in the universal sign for *please stay back*. "It's okay. I'm a nice person. Not going to hurt you or anything." I inched backward, calculating angles and distances to safety as though I hadn't failed geometry in school. Wait, were angles and distances geometry or algebra? Trigonometry? Whatever—I wasn't going to be able to use mental math to stay alive.

Then another thought hit, and I stopped moving. "How did that happen?" I pointed at the area that moments before had been a huge wall of ice.

In that instant of slipped concentration, the bear stood and ambled closer to me.

I squealed and leaped backward.

Why are you so jumpy? Don't you recognize your very own familiar when he shows up and saves you from your wonky magic?

My brain struggled to catch up. Too many ridiculous things had happened in the past twenty-four hours, and I felt a mental breakdown coming. But I couldn't have it while a polar bear stood talking to me a foot away.

The polar bear was talking to me.

"Did you... say something?"

His voice was rumbly. He didn't move his mouth, and I quickly realized the voice reverberated in my head, not through the air like a human would speak. Was this telepathy? Or had the polar bear already killed me, and my brain was shorting out?

Yeah, that second one seemed more likely. Oh! Maybe the glacier killed me, and the polar bear was sent to guide me to the next life.

I'm your familiar, he repeated, slower. *Ragnar. I'm here to protect you.* He glanced over his shoulder at the now quiet walkway. *I have some power of my own to do so with.*

"Familiar," I said out loud. I thought about Timber and relaxed a fraction. Maybe I was alive after all. My nose was so cold it hurt, which seemed to lean toward me having an earthly body still. "What ever happened to cat familiars? Nice, small, non-lethal cat familiars."

Ragnar's eyes bounced around. After a moment, I realized he'd rolled them. *Cats are great if you want sass, hairballs left all over the place, and lots of napping. Not fabulous for physical protection. Plus, they tend to like classical music, and I much prefer Reggae.*

"I see." I wasn't going to argue with the enormous bear who was talking inside my head, that was for sure. Especially about musical taste. "So you aren't going to hurt me?"

Of course not. I'm here to do the opposite—keep you safe.

"How do I know you aren't going to hurt me, like if I turn my back or something?"

He made a chuffing noise. *If I planned to eat you, I wouldn't need to wait for you to turn away. I would have already done it.* He tilted his head adorably. *But I don't usually talk to my food.*

I laughed. "So you're talking in my mind. Can I do that back to you?"

Yes. Concentrate.

I gave it a try, focusing as hard as I could and pushing thoughts toward him. *Okay. Can you hear me?*

He bobbed his head up and down. *Of course.*

Nifty. This day wasn't turning out the way I'd thought it would at all. But at least the store wasn't being bowled over by a giant glacier.

Ragnar stepped closer and extended his neck. All I could see was his massive head, and I imagined the sharp teeth in his mouth.

You can pet me if you want.

Oh. Um, thank you. I felt a quiver of fear in my belly. *Maybe another time.*

He sat back, and I was relieved for more space between us.

How are you my familiar? I mean, what makes you my familiar? Can all polar bears do this?

I made myself stop as too many questions bubbled to the surface.

Perhaps all polar bears could, but they do not all. We were invited by the spirits of the North—asked who would like to serve. I am one who volunteered, and I was given powers in return.

Wow. What kind of powers? I mean, I saw what you did with the ice wall just now. That was impressive.

Ragnar's huge head bobbed up and down slowly. *I can do some things, but I am only allowed to use magic as it relates to you, my witch. I'm tasked with helping and protecting you. And I will do so. If you should wish to slip me some gummy bears occasionally, they wouldn't be turned away.*

Tasked. What an interesting word. I wondered what it meant in this context. *Gummy bears, huh? Why that particular type of candy?*

They're my favorite.

His tone made it sound like he thought the answer was obvious.

I see. So you're sort of a cannibal then, huh?

He blinked at me with a blank expression.

Tough room. I opened my mouth to ask about the spirits of the North.

"Frankie! Make yourself look big!"

I cut my eyes to Grandpa, who had appeared in the back doorway of the general shop and shouted at me. His face was slack, and terror showed stark on his face. His gaze was on the bear, but his left hand groped for something inside of the doorway.

Ragnar turned his massive head toward Grandpa and snuffled.

Grandpa's spine jerked even straighter, and he fumbled behind the doorway faster. "Frankie, raise your arms to look big. Slowly, though. Don't make any sudden movements."

"Grandpa, I can hear this polar bear speaking in my mind. He says he's my familiar, and he saved me from a—well, a mess of a situation I got myself into." I figured Grandpa didn't need to know right that moment that I had disregarded his and Nina's advice to hold off on doing magic by myself for a while. Maybe I could somehow keep that fact hidden. One thing was for sure—I didn't plan to do it again anytime soon. A huge, hulking glacier made of ice and blood had cured me of messing around with magic before I knew quite a lot more about it.

Grandpa's Adam's apple bobbed, and his hand stopped moving as it found what it had been fumbling for. He drew a shotgun from behind the doorway.

Ragnar got to his feet and growled low.

As Grandpa brought the gun to his shoulder, I darted between the two of them and held up my hands. "No! Aren't you listening to me? He saved me. He's my familiar. I mean, he says he's my familiar, and I have no reason to doubt him, even though I thought I was dead and he was some kind of angel for a few minutes. My nose is cold, so I'm not dead. But anyway. He's saying stuff to me in my mind. Don't you dare shoot him."

"I'm not going to shoot him," Grandpa growled through gritted teeth. He raised the gun, so the barrel pointed skyward, and let off a shot.

Behind me, Ragnar roared before loping away, the dimness quickly swallowing him.

Grandpa lowered the gun but kept his eyes trained on the spot the bear had run off to. "Get inside, Frankie. He might come back."

"Am I speaking English here?" I could've sworn I'd said multiple times that Ragnar could speak in my mind, and he was my familiar. Why was my grandfather completely ignoring me and acting like a polar bear had been about to swallow me whole? "For heaven's sake, he was only sitting there, nice as any well-trained hunting dog. Don't you think he would've mauled me already if he was going to?" I was aware I was using the bear's own logic on Grandpa.

Bear logic. Huh. This day had for sure taken a ninety-degree turn.

He finally looked at me. "I heard you fine, girl. But a polar bear isn't a fitting familiar."

There was so much wrong with that statement. Like, for one thing, it wasn't as though I had actually chosen the polar bear out of a lineup of familiars. He'd simply shown up, magicked away a threat to my very existence, and then spoken telepathically into my mind. Asking only for gummy bears as payment. Leaving that aside, I simply asked, "Why?"

He turned to put the shotgun back in its place, which was, apparently, leaning against the inside door frame. I hadn't seen it there before; then again, I wasn't conditioned to look for firearms sitting around. "He's going to scare away customers if he's hanging out here all the time. Animal Control will show up—they'll tranq him and take him way out into the tundra to drop him off. He may even draw attention to Timber, and I definitely don't want him being targeted by Animal Control."

I pulled off a mitten, slid my fingers under my huge parka hood, and scratched my head. I still wasn't used to wearing fur, and it made me itchy. "Okay, I get that polar bears are huge and scary and probably shouldn't be hanging around within the Frost Peak city limits, but it isn't like I chose it. He showed up. What's going to happen now that you threatened him with a shotgun? Do I not have a familiar anymore?"

"We can hope," Grandpa grumbled. "Maybe the Arctic spirits will get their wits about them and send you something more manageable, like a snow hare." He headed toward me, and the sharp retort on my lips fell away as I saw how he hobbled. Grandpa was about seventy-six-years-old, and not having seen him for a few years, it was obvious the decline he'd undergone.

My chest ached for a moment, but I forced a smile. "I came out to clean up." I directed his attention to the area on the walkway that was now pristine. As I did, something caught my eye. "What's that?"

Grandpa stopped over the small object and peered down at it. I hurried over and knelt to pick it up, so he wouldn't try it himself. I was afraid there might be some residual ice on the walkway, and I didn't need him falling. I held a beige-colored button with an interesting herringbone pattern six inches from his eyes so he could study it better. "A button," I said unnecessarily.

His left eye twitched. "I wonder..." He trailed off.

"If this has something to do with Lloyd Dawes' death? Yeah, that's what I was thinking too. Shouldn't someone have found this when they were going over the crime scene yesterday?" By someone, I meant the town's only sheriff, who didn't even get to the crime scene until the day after the crime.

"Of course he should have, but I'm not surprised he didn't. That button would be easily missed. It's small, and it's so dark out here. Besides, Brodie's only one man. Things are different here, honey. I keep trying to tell you that."

"I'm starting to understand it." I slipped the button into my pocket and then looped an arm through my grandfather's. "Since that's the case, maybe *we* should try to figure out who killed Lloyd. We're a hundred percent better at finding clues than he is."

He shot me a grin. "Truth is, I've been working on a suspect list already."

I squeezed his arm. "Who's on it?"

He shook his head. "You first."

I certainly wasn't going to tell him that, for a hot second, I had wondered if my grandfather had killed Lloyd. After all, he would've wanted to protect his business. Lloyd was a pickpocket and had been trying to direct business away from the general store. Of course, I had dismissed the idea almost as soon as it popped into my head.

Grandpa was an old man and on the frail side. I didn't know for sure what had killed Lloyd, but I did know his skull wasn't the right shape when I found him. It had a round hole in it, maybe an inch and a half in diameter. Someone must've hit him with something hard, and I didn't think Grandpa could do that. Besides, I'd just watched him use a shotgun in the very spot I'd found Lloyd. Wouldn't he have used that if he'd killed him? "What about Aput?"

Grandpa's jaw hardened, letting me know he didn't fancy that idea. But he didn't shoot it down. Instead, he said, "What would his motive have been?"

"I'm not sure. Maybe he caught Lloyd trying to steal again or doing something sneaky in the back here or something? Where was Aput after Lloyd and I argued but before I found his body? Do you remember?"

Grandpa shook his head. "I went upstairs for a few minutes to change my clothes for the dinner we were supposed to have at Charlie's. By the time I came back down, you'd already found Lloyd."

"Yeah, that's right."

He scratched his chin with the free hand, making his beard wobble. "Aput is a good lad. He's been invaluable to me here, and I don't think he could hurt someone. He's as kind as can be to Timber, even though he doesn't know he's a familiar. Has a kind heart, that's all."

I nodded. I had only known Aput for a day and already liked him.

"Lloyd's neighbor, Carla Swanson, despised him," Grandpa said. "But she's the tip of the iceberg. I don't think his landlord liked him much, and there were others."

"That's what Nina said—Lloyd had a lot of enemies. Did anyone around here actually like him?"

Grandpa shrugged. "His sister Molly, maybe? But like would probably be a strong word. I don't think they were real close." He pulled me forward. "We'll freeze to death if we stand here talking about each of the people in this town who had motive to kill Lloyd Dawes. He was not a well-liked man."

"I'm beginning to understand that. The problem is I got the feeling the sheriff thinks I had motive to kill him. Because we argued shortly before his death, and plenty of people saw it." I leaned my head on his shoulder for a second. "Let's get inside." I looked around, hoping to get a final glimpse of Ragnar, but it was too dim to see far. Still, I got the odd feeling of being watched.

Wait a minute. Feeling watched. Ragnar was the bear at the airport! And he must have been hanging around watching me when I had that strange feeling before going into the store the first time.

I wasn't sure how to feel about that.

Aput had opened the store while Grandpa and I were out back, and there were two customers inside already. I hurried to get my parka off and met one of them right as he arrived at the checkout counter with his items.

"Will this be all, sir?"

"Yep. And that's more than I planned to get here today. I almost went over to Breckenridge for my supplies after I heard you folks may be murdering customers around this place. Maybe that new place in Cross Creek'll go up soon, and we can all shop somewhere safer." He drew his lips back in a parody of a grin, revealing yellowed and cracked front teeth.

I gaped, unable to figure out what to say.

"You oughta know better than that, Stan," Grandpa called from near the ammunition. "Happened outside, and none of us were involved. Won't be long before Brodie figures out who did it. No reason for you to be trekking to Breckenridge and risking getting hurt. We can handle your supply needs right here like we always have."

Stan shut his mouth, paid, and left, but I stewed. If that guy had considered going to another town for his supplies, others might be thinking about or even doing the same thing. And what was that about a new store opening?

What were we going to do? The business couldn't absorb much of a hit to its income.

So many things were going on that it was hard for me to pin down my whirling thoughts.

What was I going to do about being a suspect in Lloyd Dawes' death? And about folks in town thinking it wasn't safe to shop with us?

And Grandpa hadn't reacted well to Ragnar. What was I going to do about that?

Wait, what was I going to do about being a witch and having a polar bear familiar in the first place?

I dropped my chin to my chest. Silly old me had thought the worst problem I'd have moving to Frost Peak would be the lack of opportunity to wear my favorite bikini.

Lifting my chin, I straightened my shoulders and decided the first thing I'd have to do was figure out who killed Lloyd Dawes. I couldn't wait for Brodie to get around to it. By then, the townsfolk might have driven us out of business.

Nope. If our names were going to be cleared, I was going to have to clear them myself.

Chapter 5

The topic of the day among customers as they came and left Spitzer's General Store was Lloyd Dawes' murder, which made sense in a way, but in another way it shocked me. I wondered if I'd ever get used to living in such a small town, where everyone knew everyone's business almost immediately. It certainly wasn't that way in the city where I'd lived in California.

The secondary topic of the day was what the new store in Cross Creek would be like and whether people would need to go there from now on if a killer was working at Spitzer's. Whenever I heard those rumblings, my gut twisted.

Around midmorning, Sheriff Brodie entered the store and made a beeline for me. Nerves twittered in my stomach as I wondered what he was doing there.

"Can I talk to you in the back?" He jerked his chin toward the supply room.

"Sure, come on." I led him to the back, where Aput was moving some boxes from place to place. I smiled at the young man. "The sheriff here wants to talk to me alone. Would you mind manning the checkout counter for a few minutes?"

Aput nodded good-naturedly. "Sure thing. By the way, we're low on hunting knives. George ordered some a few weeks ago, but they haven't gotten here yet, and we're down to only a few on the floor."

I frowned. "Why are they taking so long to get here?"

"Everything takes a long time to get here. We don't have a big airport, and trucks going over land sometimes get blocked by bad weather." He headed for the door but stopped and turned back. "Um, I don't know if I should mention this, but there's a better place we could be ordering from. I tried to talk to your grandfather about it, but he wasn't interested."

"Oh, yeah?" I was puzzled. Why wouldn't Grandpa want to work with a more reliable supplier?

Brodie cleared his throat. Oh, right. I was supposed to be talking to him. I smiled at Aput again. "How about you and I talk about this new supply place soon? Maybe I can get Grandpa to change his mind about it."

Aput brightened. "Sounds good, Frankie. Thanks."

The sheriff and I watched the young man leave, and then I turned toward him. "What do you need?"

"The coroner ruled that Lloyd was killed by blunt force trauma. Do you know what the weapon could've been?"

I crossed my arms. "Why would I know that?"

His fingers tapped at the butt of the pistol on his belt. "You're the one who found him. I wondered if you might have seen the weapon."

"Of course not. If I had, I would have left it right there with the body. There was no weapon around when I found him. Of course, it's dark all the time here, and it was dark then. I suppose it could've skidded away, but then you would've found it when you looked out there, or the medical people would have when they came and got the body, right?"

Brodie didn't answer. Instead, he asked another question. "Do you have any idea who killed Lloyd?"

"No, but to hear the people around here talk, a better question might be who *wouldn't* have killed him. I mean, seems like the guy had a ton of enemies, and lots of people didn't want him around anymore."

Brodie nodded, cocking his jaw as he scrutinized me. I shifted my weight, wishing he would look somewhere else.

After a tense silence that lasted too long, he said, "I'm going to be gone for a few days. I have to transport a prisoner to authorities farther south."

My jaw dropped. "Are you serious? We just had a murder in Frost Peak, and you're telling me we're going to be left without law enforcement for a few days?"

"Actually, it's at *least* a few days. Could be more."

I couldn't think of what to say, so I shook my head and made a series of noises meant to convey my shock.

Brodie chuckled. "Look, you've heard of the Wild West, right? It's the Wild North up here. Sorry, but I'm one man. The community has to come together and police itself in my absence. It's not ideal, but it's the way it is."

"Police ourselves," I repeated in disbelief. What kind of place had I brought myself to? What kind of place did my grandfather live in? And Nina and Aput. I hadn't known them long, but I already cared about them, and I was sure there were loads of other people in this community I would care about once I got to know them. I wanted them all to live in a safe place.

Brodie's casual statement about what life was like in Frost Peak flabbergasted me, for sure, but I was struck that I didn't feel more *frightened* about it. I found myself thinking about Ragnar, and how he had promised to protect me.

I dragged my mind back to the arrogant guy in front of me. How did someone manage to strike a cocky swagger when they were simply standing there? "Do you have a suspect at the top of your list? Besides me, I mean."

He wrinkled his nose and then rubbed it as though something had tickled it. "His neighbor, Carla Swanson, has called me out several times—the two of them had an ongoing feud. If I had time before I needed to leave, that's where I'd start. But the only reason I'm telling you that is so you'll know I'm working on it. You shouldn't do anything with that information or go near any suspects. For now, you're still a suspect yourself."

"So why'd you come by here, then? If you want me to be in the dark about the investigation, why come in and tell me about the murder weapon?"

His chest rose and fell on a deep breath. "You had to already know Lloyd was hit by something because you found the body. I'm sure you saw the two-inch, round wound that caved in his skull. I'm not letting the information about the murder weapon out to the public at large. And you're a suspect, yes. You have to be. You found the body, but no one else was around. Plus, you had a public argument. But I'm also concerned about you and your grandfather. I want you to keep your wits about you, and keep your eyes open."

"You think Grandpa and I are in danger?"

"I think there's a killer in Frost Peak, and *everybody* here should keep an eye out for anything unusual. But, yes, the murder happened on your property, and I think that may be significant." He turned to walk away and shot over his shoulder, "See you in a few days, Ms. Banks. Stay out of trouble. I'd hate to have to transport *you* to the authorities after I'm done with this trip."

A snarky response jumped to my lips, but I was too busy watching his attractive retreat to spit it out.

I shook my head and screwed my eyes shut. What in the world? Brodie was insufferable, so why was I noticing how good-looking he was? Surely, I hadn't been in this tiny town long enough to get to the point Nina was at, where she'd go after any man who was the slightest bit attractive.

I rolled my neck and waited a few minutes, not wanting to run into Brodie again out front. I thought about what the sheriff had said about Lloyd's neighbor. It wasn't the first mention I'd heard of Carla, and I was more than a little intrigued about the feud between her and Lloyd.

When I ventured out, Aput caught me right away. He handed me a brochure. "This is the supply company I was telling you about. I've been researching them for a few months, and I'm convinced they have a better process for getting things to us. They bring stuff to a closer city than the company your grandfather works with before taking a smaller plane to Frost Peak. That smaller plane company has some super reliable pilots with a fantastic track record of making deadlines, even during the rough seasons. They're treated well and get bonuses routinely for doing well. They're motivated and very good pilots."

I couldn't help but smile at his eager puppy dog look. I glanced through the brochure. "That's a lot of homework you've done on this company. You feel pretty strongly about this."

Aput ducked his head and nodded.

"It's great that you care enough about the store to spend time outside of work doing stuff like this." I waved the brochure. "I'm going to recommend to Grandpa that we switch to this company."

His head jerked up, and dark eyes searched my face. "Thanks." His chest puffed out, and he carried himself straighter as he went back to work.

I grinned at his back. Grandpa sure had found a gem of a guy to work for him. I was going to convince him he needed to listen and be receptive to Aput's ideas about improving the place.

The next couple of hours went by quickly as I waited on customers, helped Aput stock, and took a quick snack break in the apartment. I didn't find time to talk to my grandfather about the supply company —he was as busy as me, chatting away to clients and helping them pick out supplies. He was fantastic at small talk, and his kind smile made people open up to him.

More than once, I heard him talk down someone who was afraid I was a killer and maybe they shouldn't shop here anymore. It made me feel good to see how well-respected my grandfather was in the community.

Right when I was starting to dream about lunch, Grandpa sidled up to me. "That's Carla Swanson coming in."

I followed the direction his eyes were fixed through the front windows to find a bundled-up woman approaching. She carried a gnarled walking stick and wore mukluk style boots.

Right away, I noticed Carla didn't have an aura. Since my brain had opened up to the idea, I could see the auras all the time. I'd noticed them on many of the day's customers.

Nina had said only a couple of women in town weren't witches, and this was obviously one.

My eyes darted around the place, looking for any indications of magic I might need to get rid of before she entered. Then I chuckled. Why would there be anything like that around? It wasn't like we did magic willy-nilly in the store all day.

There was so much to get used to.

Carla entered and shook snow off herself onto the entryway mat before lowering her parka hood and looking around. Her nose was bright red, and her cheeks matched. She pulled off her mittens, holding the walking stick in the crook of her arm as she did.

My brain twirled around. Should I talk to Carla about Lloyd? Maybe their feud had motivated her to kill him? That walking stick looked heavy and substantial. Plenty of potential for blunt force trauma, as the sheriff had put it.

Carla wiped her feet a few times and trudged forward. I hurried to greet her with a chipper, "Welcome to Spitzer's General Store!"

She eyed me with suspicion. "I've been coming here for decades and never got a welcome like that. What, did George hire one of them greeters like they have in big stores in the lower forty-eight or something?"

I shook my head and delivered a bright smile. "I'm Frankie Banks, George's granddaughter. I've moved to Frost Peak to help him with the store."

She let out a sound I thought could be made by an irritable moose and pushed past me. "He could use more help. There's never enough of anything, so I assume he could use someone to do the ordering for him."

I glanced at Grandpa, who was situated so he was behind Carla. He made a face at the back of her head, then winked at me and wandered into the next row to help Aput straighten the snacks.

"I'll certainly be looking into that. What's your name? I'm trying to learn everyone, but I apologize in advance if I forget."

"Carla Swanson." She looked at a magazine and then tossed it back onto the rack, sideways.

"Oh, I've heard your name. You live out on Starling Street, right?"

Her eyes darted to pin me with a suspicious look. "Yeah. How'd you know that?"

With a shrug, I hurried to cover my tracks. "Nina Montes has been trying to get me up to speed on folks I should know about. In fact, she's taking me to some party or something to introduce me around later. I remember she said you live on Starling because it's the same street as the late Lloyd Dawes." My fingers twitched—I wanted to straighten the magazine she'd left so disheveled but resisted.

"Lloyd," Carla spat. "What a rat. He was my next-door neighbor. Emphasis on the was, and I'm glad for it."

I cleared my throat and followed her as she thumped over to the frozen foods section. "So the two of you didn't get along? Wasn't he a very good neighbor?"

"The worst. Unless you think living next to someone who pees in your snow every day—to make colored ice sculptures, he always said— is a good neighbor." She scanned the shelves and harrumphed when whatever she wanted was missing. Whirling toward me, she demanded, "When will you get some decent frozen vegetables in here? It's the dark season, and I'm running out of canned beans."

"I'll put it on my list and get on it as soon as possible. And to answer your other question, no, I wouldn't think someone who... did what you said was a good neighbor."

Her expression softened an iota. "You'd be right. And I suppose you'd also think it was a bad neighbor who played loud, banging, metal music five out of seven nights until one am. Or who dumped his trash in the back corner of your lawn weekly because he was too cheap to pay for trash removal." She thumped her stick twice on the floor to punctuate her complaints.

"That's... that sounds horrible. Couldn't the police have helped you with that situation? Some of it sounds illegal."

She tipped her head back and howled with laughter. When she finally stopped to catch her breath, she leaned to look around me and hollered, "George, you'd better have a talk with this girl about how things are around here."

"I've tried!" he called back, invisible in a deeper aisle. "Girl's stubborn."

She straightened to pin me with bright green eyes. "Brodie came out at least a dozen times during the few years I lived next to Lloyd. Never did anything other than tell him to mind his manners." She zigged around me, this time heading for the canned goods aisle. "So I had to handle it myself."

Herself? I scooted after her. "What do you mean?"

"I mean I did everything I could to get Lloyd to move away or to get him into some real trouble. Never could manage it, though. In fact, his own landlord wanted him out." She picked up a can of pickled beets and peered at the label.

"Who was his landlord?"

"Mickey Grimes. He's my landlord too. He visited me about a year ago and said to let him know if I figured out a way to get Lloyd out." She set the beets down with a frown and picked up some canned potatoes.

I was beginning to wonder whether Carla was going to buy anything. "Why did Mickey want him out?"

"Because he didn't take care of the property." She cast me a look that let me know she thought I was rather dumb for asking. "Now that Lloyd is gone, it'll take half a year to clean the place up enough for someone else to live in it. Lloyd even tried to build an underground bunker in the back yard but only managed to dig a hole till he hit the permafrost. Then he lost interest and left it there."

"I see. That does sound like a lot of work for Mickey." I grabbed a can of stewed tomatoes and offered them up for Carla's consideration.

She shook her head at the tomatoes and put the potatoes back too. Then she turned toward me. "I'm glad Lloyd's dead. Now I don't have to worry about any of his madness."

Before giving it much thought, I blurted out, "Where were you the day he died between five-thirty and six?"

She squinted and thumped her walking stick a couple times. "Home having a TV dinner and watching Matlock. Why?"

That wasn't a good alibi, right? She had no one to verify if she was alone. "No reason. Is there anything I can help you find?"

"Bah. As usual, I'm going to have to settle for stuff I don't like. Get me a cart, will you?"

"Of course." I hustled to get it for her, then busied myself tidying until she was ready to check out. After she'd paid, I gave her a sunny smile and wished her a good evening.

A snort was her only reply as she plodded off, pushing the cart to the exit, then grabbing her bags out of it and leaving.

"Wow, Carla didn't like Lloyd much, huh?" Aput appeared from behind a display he'd been working on.

"Heard that, did you?"

He nodded. "I was hiding from her. Sorry about that."

I giggled. "I'm sure you've dealt with her before. It was my turn."

"I'll tell you what I heard," Grandpa said, coming out of the back room. "I heard you digging for information about the murder." He didn't look or sound happy about it.

"I wanted to know what she and Lloyd used to argue about, that's all." I opened the cash drawer to start counting it down to close up shop. "I'm curious."

"Listen, honey. There's a murderer on the loose in Frost Peak. I want you to keep your head down. Stay out of it. Let Brodie handle it."

I flashed him an irritated look. "Let Brodie handle it in a few days when he gets back, you mean? That seems like a terrible idea."

"I know it does to you, but that's only because you aren't used to things here yet."

"Pretty sure I'm never going to get used to having a police department that is never available to do police work." When he glared at me, I addressed Aput. "This Mickey Grimes. He's a big landlord around here or something?"

Aput shrugged. "He owns some places, yeah. He's more a developer, though. Likes to build things and turn buildings into other things. I don't know if Carla knows it, but if you ask me, the reason he wanted Lloyd out of that house wasn't because he was messy. It was because Mickey wanted to make a small hotel on that land."

I tried to imagine people coming here on vacation. Sure, the place was ruggedly beautiful, and I suspected it might be kind of cool in the summer, but was there enough to do to draw much tourism? And what about wintertime? Seemed like it would be sitting there not making any money then. "Interesting," I mused.

"Stop being interested in stuff that's not related to this store and your life," Grandpa advised with a gruff tone. "Seems to me you have enough on your plate getting used to certain things here without adding other people's problems to your to-do list." He gave me a knowing look.

I knew he was talking about getting used to the fact that I could work magic. And he was right. That *was* enough to worry about. But I was a suspect in Lloyd's murder, and Brodie wasn't making good progress figuring out a more likely suspect, so I was going to have to do it and get used to being a witch at the same time.

I nodded, and Grandpa headed upstairs.

Aput watched him go, then said quietly, "I'd stay away from Mickey if I were you."

"Oh, yeah? Why's that?"

"He has a bad reputation. I don't know if any of it's true or if it's just chatter, but folks say his wife is dead, even though he says she's in Florida."

My eyebrows climbed into my hairline. "You mean, people think he killed her?"

"Some folks do, yeah. Plus, he has a record. He's been to prison for racketeering. He came here when he got out of prison for that. People say he got the money to get started here from guys he knew in prison." He shook his head. "My mama told me to stay away from Mickey, that he's not the kind of guy you want to cross."

"I see. Thanks, Aput."

He nodded and headed for the back room.

The bells went off over the front door, and Nina breezed in. "Ready to go, Cali-girl?"

"Almost."

Grandpa reappeared on the stairway. "Where are you two heading?"

"I offered to take her to the Founder's Day celebration over at the community center tonight." Nina pushed her hood back.

"Oh, yeah? How'd you convince her to go to that?"

I cocked my head. "Why wouldn't I go? Nina said it would be a good way to meet lots of people at once."

He rubbed his chin, making the long beard twitch. "And that convinced you?"

Nina chimed in. "Nope. I got nowhere with that line of reasoning. So I told her they're going to have a huge, four-tier cake, and she couldn't agree to come fast enough."

"Ah!" Grandpa grinned widely. "My girl loves her sweets."

"I still don't get why there's no bakery here," I grumped, pouting.

"Too hard to keep a steady stream of that type of ingredient," he explained. "Hey, if there's cake, maybe Aput and I'll come too, once we're all done here." He nudged me away from the cash register. "I'll finish this. You go along with Nina and have fun."

"Thanks." I grabbed my parka and mittens and followed Nina out the front door.

I was grateful to escape because I was pretty sure my grandfather would have picked back up on the lecture about digging into the investigation. And I loved the man, but I wasn't going to sit by and leave our business and possibly my freedom at risk.

Chapter 6

The cake was all I'd hoped it would be—enormous with fluffy but only lightly sweet frosting, and each layer was a different flavor. I hadn't gotten too far away from it for the first half hour, too worried I'd miss the cutting. Nina had been annoyed and tried to get me to mingle, play some games, and have other food. But I'd stood firm until they cut the cake and I got my share.

Yes, three pieces was a reasonable amount for one person's share. I was willing to argue with anyone on that point. Who knew when the next time I'd get cake would be?

"Wow. You can really put away the sugar," Nina marveled. Bafflingly, she'd only eaten two bites of her micro piece of cake before pushing the plate away.

"I'm so tired of smoked fish and canned vegetables," I said around my last bite. "And I didn't even know until I moved here that people eat walrus."

"You've been here threedays. That's not enough time to get tired of any kind of food."

I eyed the dessert table, contemplating getting a fourth piece. My stomach lurched in protest.

"You're a bit green right now. Are you going to be sick?" Nina backed away, as though afraid I might lose my cake in her direction.

"No. But I could use some water."

"Come on. Let's walk around. We'll get you a bottle of water, and the exercise should help you digest." She pulled me up and hauled me over to get a water from one of the multiple coolers by the food table.

We wandered around the room, which was a big rectangle, like most community center event rooms. A DJ took requests in the far corner while people danced. But there was no way I could dance with a gut full of sweets.

People played rousing games of corn hole in another corner of the room, and we stopped to watch for a few minutes. Several tables full of people played bingo while they munched refreshments. I was shocked more people weren't diving into that cake.

A silent auction table held a variety of themed baskets, and I bid on a movie night at home one and another full of romance novels. At the end of the table was a jar of buttons and a second jar for putting in a guess for how many there were. The closest person would win a gift certificate to One Buck Louise's, which Nina told me was a thrift shop in town.

The buttons reminded me of the one Grandpa and I had found near where Lloyd's body was.

"You!" The word was a shriek, and I spun around, expecting to see that a row had started over bingo or something.

But a woman strode toward us, and her finger pointed right at me. I tapped my chest. "Me?"

"Yes, you!" She stopped a few feet from me and crossed her arms. The forty-something woman had a crook in the middle of her nose and a wide jaw and forehead with thin, chin-length, dirty blonde hair that was thinner on the top and sides, like a non-chosen mullet. She wore a pair of round-rimmed glasses much too big for her face, and her aura was beginning to appear.

I recognized her. She was in the store when I first arrived. When Lloyd was there. She was in the fishing aisle when I was trying to get him to stop harassing people with his flyers.

"You killed my brother." She spat out the words surprisingly loud.

So loudly, in fact, that I saw all kinds of heads spin around in our direction. The bingo caller gaped at us, forgetting to shout the next tile.

My gaze returned to the angry woman still staring at me. Now I could see the resemblance to Lloyd Dawes, though this woman's face was fuller. Less gaunt. "I'm sorry. Who are you?"

"Frankie Banks," Nina said, "this is Molly Dawes." She gave an arm flourish that reminded me of a butler announcing a guest in a grand hall.

Molly ignored her. "You had a fight with my brother right before he wound up dead."

"Both of those things are true, but I didn't kill him. I found him dead." My gaze darted around. The noise level in the room had decreased. People looked in our direction. Bingo was still on hold.

Molly noticed people watching too. It didn't stop her, though. "He was the only family I had left. Now I'm all alone in the world. An orphan and whatever they call people who've lost all their siblings. Because of you."

"I didn't even think she liked her brother," Nina said, close to my ear.

Ignoring Nina, I focused on Molly. "I understand this must be a hard time for you, but again, I didn't do anything other than try to get your brother to return a bunch of stuff he had shoplifted from my family's store."

"So you killed him for a few cheap items? That's all his life was worth to you?" Her face twisted in disgust.

"I didn't say—"

"Molly, is this the one you were telling me about?" A tall man with a hefty mid-section stepped up next to Molly. "Is this the person who hit Lloyd over the head and killed him?"

"That's quite an accusation, Mickey," Nina said.

Mickey? "Mickey Grimes? Lloyd's landlord?" I asked.

He didn't answer, his attention on Molly, who nodded. "Yes, she admits she was mad that Lloyd pocketed a couple of cheap-o things from her precious store."

"I don't think they were all that cheap." I shook my head to clear it. This conversation was devolving faster than I could keep up. "Listen, Lloyd was shoplifting, and I didn't like that. But I didn't kill him. I'm not under arrest, right? Sheriff Brodie didn't find any evidence to charge me with the murder."

Molly and Mickey gave identical scoffs. "Sheriff Brodie doesn't have time to actually investigate cases," Mickey said. "He leaves that to Frost Peak's residents. And all the residents I've talked to think you're the likeliest suspect."

Indignation rolled over me. "Why? Because I disagreed with him doing something illegal right in front of me?" I balled my fists. "Funny, the folks I've talked to seem to think it's anybody's guess who killed Lloyd because he had so many enemies." I remembered Aput's warning, too late. This could probably be considered crossing Mickey, right? I wasn't supposed to do that—he might have killed his wife, had been in prison, and used dirty money to fund his life in Frost Peak.

Oops.

Murmurs, both of assent and dissent, traveled through the room behind me. I realized the music was now silent too. Seemed like everyone in town was watching these two confront me.

Okay. I needed to get ahold of myself. Screaming at these folks defensively wasn't going to help my cause. It would only paint the picture with even broader strokes that I was a nut who might kill in anger.

I forced a smile. "I'm so sorry, again, for your loss. I understand how difficult it must be to not know who's to blame for your brother's death. You need closure, I'm sure. I hope you get it."

Turning away, I grabbed Nina's arm. She shot a glare at Mickey and Molly before coming along with me. I headed straight for the door, feeling the heaviness of dozens of eyes on me. I concentrated on walking and keeping my chin from sinking to my chest.

When we were outside with the door closed behind us, I drew a deep breath.

"That was intense," Nina said.

"Yeah. I mean, I knew I was on the suspect list, but it was pretty harsh being directly accused. And by Lloyd's family too." We shuffled down the sidewalk, covered by an inch of snow that had fallen while we were inside. "I guess the whole town thinks I'm a murderer, huh?"

"I don't."

I shot Nina a grateful look. "I guess it's easier to suspect the newcomer nobody knows well, huh?"

She nodded. "Frost Peak can be a tight-knit place. Folks have to stick together to survive up here. But they had no call to accuse you like that in public."

We were silent for a few minutes, and my thoughts wandered back over the conversation. Suddenly, I stopped.

Nina went a few more steps before realizing I wasn't keeping pace. "What's up?"

"Mickey Grimes asked if I was the one who'd hit Lloyd over the head, but Sheriff Brodie told me he wasn't letting that information out into the general community. How did Mickey know the cause of death?"

Nina pursed her lips, then started walking again. "That's a very good question. Hey, you're kind of like one of those people in books and movies who aren't law enforcement but who solve crimes. What are they called again?"

"Sleuths?" I guessed as I hurried to catch up to her. "I don't want to be a sleuth," I insisted. "But I do want to find out who killed Lloyd so I can finish getting settled in this town without everybody thinking I'm a killer."

She nodded, and we walked in silence. I didn't know what she was thinking about, but I was mulling over how to figure out whether Lloyd Dawes' landlord had killed him.

A plan hatched in my mind quickly. Now I had to get Nina to agree to help me.

Chapter 7

"So, let me get this straight. You want to commit breaking and entering into Lloyd Dawes' house. And you want me to be there in case getting in requires magic?"

"Yes, you got it right," I said sheepishly. It sounded shadier when she said it out loud than it had in my head. I held my breath and waited for her to chastise my plan to do something illegal.

Nina was quiet for a moment, and then she gave a shrug and said, "Okay, I'm in."

"You are?" My voice headed upward on the last word.

"Yep. I don't much care about all this, but I like you. I don't think you killed Lloyd, and I've also been around Frost Peak long enough to know it could take Jason Brodie several months to get it figured out on his own—spending months under everyone's suspicion is going to turn enough people's opinions of you south to make it hard to regain folks' respect after that."

"Thanks. I appreciate the vote of confidence and the help." I let us in the back door of the store so we could plan our investigative trip to Dawes' house. Nina thought it was a good idea to go right away, so we wouldn't risk Brodie getting back and checking it out first, maybe removing something we could use for evidence.

But no sooner were we inside that Nina's cell phone buzzed. She picked it up and chatted for a few minutes before hanging up and turning a pained expression toward me. "I have to cancel on you, Cali-girl. That was my boss over at the airport. An unexpected shipment is coming in tonight—lots of stuff for your store, actually. I have to go over there and work."

I groaned, but the disappointment I felt was quickly pushed away by eagerness over the shipment. It was never a bad thing to be getting more supplies for the store, especially right now, while we were fighting for goodwill among our customers. Plus, this particular shipment included some baking supplies Grandpa told me he'd ordered when he knew I was coming. I was eager to have sugar, flour, and vanilla around for a little while. "I understand." I sank into the chair behind the checkout counter and pushed with my feet to spin myself around a few times.

Nina eyed me suspiciously. "Don't go by yourself. It's after dark and too dangerous to travel, for one thing. For another, you can't use magic to break in, so it will take you longer, and you might get caught."

I shook my head. "I'm not going to go by myself. I understand."

I waved her back into the cold outdoors and started to climb the stairs. I knew Grandpa was most likely watching some old Western or mystery, and I would try to busy myself reading or drawing in my sketchbook.

At the foot of the steps, I paused. Maybe I *should* go to Dawes' place. After all, things were heating up more with folks accusing me in public. Plus, Nina was right about the fact that Brodie wasn't going to be able to solve this case very quickly. The experience I'd had at the Founder's Day celebration was horrible, and I didn't want to go through it again anytime soon.

I thought about how people had come into the store saying they were thinking about shopping elsewhere too. The longer it took to solve this case, the more problems I was going to have, and that could even spill over into less business for the store.

Nope. I had to do something. I spun around, pulled my parka back on, and zipped into the back room to get one of Grandpa's radios. I was proud of myself for remembering he'd told me I should always take a radio when going out on a snowmobile. There was never any guarantee that cell phones would work when you weren't right in the heart of town. It was hit or miss.

Before stepping out into the night, I googled Dawes' address, thinking the whole thing would be a nonstarter if it wasn't there. I knew the street was Starling but had no idea what the number was.

The first entry was Dawes' website for prepper supplies, and it had his address at the bottom. With a soft whoop of victory and a fair amount of surprise that he hadn't used a PO box for the site, I punched the address into my maps app and studied it for a few minutes. Once I was reasonably sure I had the route memorized, I pulled on my thick mittens and went out the back door.

Grandpa's snowmobiles were in a shed behind the main building. I pawed for the keys on the hook and chose the machine that went with the first set I grabbed.

For a moment, I worried Grandpa would hear the snowmobile and try to stop me, but I made myself relax. The sound of snowmobiles was pretty constant around here unless it was the dead of night. Likely, he wouldn't think twice about hearing one go by the store. Especially since he always played his Westerns at near top volume.

According to my app, Dawes' place was about fifteen minutes away, so I settled in and gunned it once I was beyond the thickest part of town. There was a worn snowmobile track, and confidence flowed through me as I followed it by the light of the headlamp. I had learned a lot in the incredibly short time I'd lived in Frost Peak. Maybe it'd been a good move for me after all. I could be a natural at living in the far north.

The first time the snowmobile sputtered, I stiffened in my seat, and a little thrill of fear skittered up and down my spine. I swallowed hard and tried to convince myself I'd imagined it as my heart thudded away at top speed. But in the next moment, the machine lost power, sputtered a few more times, and glided to a stop. It only took an instant for me to realize my mistake—it was out of gas. "Oh, no, no, no. Why am I so stupid?" I groped around in my parka pocket for the radio. Now I was going to have to call Grandpa or Aput or someone to ride out and get me. And how was I going to explain what I was doing out here in the first place?

I groaned, hit the radio's on button, and watched the lights blink on. But as soon as I tried to move the dial to get a decent channel, it went completely dark and refused to respond when I repeatedly hit the power button. I dropped my head back to stare at the stars, a frustrated scream gathering in my chest.

I hadn't checked the radio's battery. All that self-talk about how I was getting good at living in the Alaskan wilderness danced around in my brain, stabbing at me gleefully. I was actually, perhaps, the most ridiculously stupid person to *ever* live in the wilderness.

What was I going to do?

I looked around. It'd gotten even darker since I'd set out. The light snow falling meant clouds blocked much of the starlight. It was also colder than before.

I didn't have a choice. I couldn't sit there and wait for someone to come along because I had no idea when that would happen.

Could I do some magic to get this machine going? I lifted my head and contemplated it, even thinking about what I could for a rhyme.

Then the image of the huge glacier behind Grandpa's store jumped into my mind. I couldn't do magic. I didn't know enough yet. I had to walk back.

I hauled myself off the machine, thinking about how I'd have to come back and get it the next day, with a gas can. Which would probably involve telling my grandfather what I'd done. My face burned with shame at the mere thought.

I pulled the parka hood closer over the sides of my face, stuck the radio back in my pocket, and began to trudge.

It quickly became apparent it was going to be a hard walk without any light. A quick check of my phone let me know it wasn't going to provide a flashlight for very long because it only had about a quarter of its battery life. I was beginning to see a theme to this ill-fated trip. I decided to save the phone's battery in case I got close enough to town that it would work. I stuffed it inside the pocket of my parka to keep it warm and concentrated on walking slowly to stay in the snowmobile's path.

It was still snowing, and fear struck at my chest. What if the tracks got filled in, and I got turned around? I'd be in real danger almost immediately.

I inched along, fighting back panic and wishing I had waited for Nina.

Then I heard something that, in less than a second, made my fear escalate to terror and attempt to freeze me from the inside out.

It was a low growl.

I stopped and stilled my body, though there was no way I could ease back my heart rate even a tiny bit.

Something dark moved at my periphery. I choked back a scream and stayed still, begging my eyes to focus better in the dimness.

A second growl pierced the night from my other side, and a snuffle at my back let me know I was surrounded. Incrementally, I turned my head to see the creature at my right, whose noises let me know it was the closest.

My absolute worst fear was confirmed as my gaze fell on a snarling, drooling creature out of storybooks that were meant to warn child-Frankie and others like her against going off on stupid adventures like this one.

Wolf.

Actually, it was *wolves*, but the primal horror in my brain shied away from the knowledge that I was surrounded by a pack of hungry creatures.

What should I do? I didn't have a weapon. Nothing that would maim or scare these wild animals. No fire. Nothing that would make a loud noise other than my own voice, which felt at the moment as though the most it could possibly do was squeak, weak as a newborn.

I widened my stance, beat down my fear to as manageable a level as possible, and gripped the radio in one hand and cell phone in the other, preparing to fight for my life.

Chapter 8

The closest wolf crouched, focusing yellow eyes on me. I gripped the radio tighter but knew that knocking the animal in the head with it would likely do nothing but infuriate him.

In an instant, he launched for my neck. I raised my arms and braced my feet for the impact.

But it never came. A thunderous roar erupted, tearing through the air as a massive shape smashed into the wolf's side, hurtling it off into the night in a high arc.

Ragnar stood on his hind legs in front of me and roared again, shaking his head back and forth as though to keep his eyes on all the wolves at once. My ears, already ringing from the first bellow, throbbed painfully. I slapped my hands over them and watched in awe as the polar bear swung his head from side to side again, snarling and snapping as spittle flew from his mouth.

The wolves slunk away, the one Ragnar had bashed into moving more slowly, with an obvious limp.

When the pack was out of sight, Ragnar dropped to all fours and turned to face me. *Are you hurt?*

I shook my head and swallowed hard, slowly dropping my hands, still holding the ridiculous faux weapons. "I'm fine. But I think you hurt that wolf."

Ragnar sniffed the air. *Would you have rather I let them make you their dinner?* His voice rumbled around in my head.

"No!" I cried. Softer, I said, "No. I'm sorry." I screwed my eyes shut and then snapped them open when all I saw behind the lids was a snarling wolf. "Life's rough in the Great White North, isn't it?"

It's rough, indeed. Which is exactly why you need me. To protect you, both when you make blunders that put you in danger and when you're threatened by no fault of your own.

I winced. Feeling too overwrought to focus on speaking to him telepathically, I continued out loud. There was no one around to hear anyway. "Tonight was my own blundering. A series of them, really. I was stupid a few times over."

Ragnar tipped his head. *Tell me.*

"I decided to take a trip out to Lloyd Dawes' house. People in Frost Peak think I killed him, and Sheriff Brodie is gone, so there's no one to figure out who the real killer is besides me. Nina was supposed to come help me, but she got called in to work. I took a snowmobile," I jerked a thumb behind me, "but it ran out of gas, and the radio I brought died too. So I was trying to walk home without losing my way."

Ragnar chuffed and snuffled. I was starting to recognize those noises as laughter.

I zipped my lips, even though I wanted to say something snarky. Even though I knew I'd been an idiot, I didn't like being laughed at.

The bear looked me in the eye. *Would you like me to take you to Lloyd's house?*

That was not what I'd expected him to say. "How?"

Since you aren't a cub, I can't grab you by the scruff of the neck. His tone held sarcasm. *On my back, of course.*

Ride a polar bear? I'd never even ridden a horse. But it wasn't like I could hail a cab or anything. It was either give it a try or walk. And I did want to go to Lloyd's place instead of heading back home and having this whole ridiculous thing be a waste of time. Plus, I might not make it walking home. I hadn't allowed my mind to go there before, but there was a real chance I'd get too tired and weak or cold before I made it.

Besides, Ragnar had come barreling to my aid twice now. He wasn't out to hurt me. I nodded. "But how do I get up there?"

He sat down, rear legs jutting in front of his body. *Grab my neck fur and center yourself, then hold tight.*

How was I supposed to do that with my heavy mittens? I stepped forward, tentative. I slipped my mittens off, shoved them into my parka's pockets, and grabbed two handfuls of rough fur, one at each of the bear's shoulders. As much as possible, I centered myself on my tiptoes and held my breath.

With an oof, Ragnar slowly stood. I squealed, throwing my hips to the left as my body tried to lurch off his right side. I used my knees to get balanced and then, suddenly, I was up. As fast as possible, I pulled the mittens back on and then patted Ragnar to let him know I was as ready as possible.

In my mind, he said, *Use your knees to stay on. I'll go slowly.*

In the next instant, he surged forward, loping along, his stride eating up big sections of land. Not sure he'd hear me if I spoke aloud, I focused and hollered into his mind, *That's not slow!*

He chuff-laughed in my thoughts. *It is for me. Hold tighter.*

There was no way to squeeze more with my knees, so I leaned forward, hugging with my arms. As Ragnar ran, I felt his muscles flex and lengthen. He smelled faintly of fish but mostly of snow and wide-open spaces, and his fur was shockingly soft against my face.

It surprised me to realize I wasn't afraid anymore. I felt something way different from fear. What was it?

The only sounds were Ragnar's breaths and the thudding of his massive paws on the snow. The only thing I could see was the dim night and his fur in front of my eyes. The only thing I felt was the earth falling away behind us, and it felt like I'd always imagined flying would feel.

Oh, yes. I recognized the feeling now. Exhilaration.

"Thank you." I slid off Ragnar's back, then he rose to his feet again.

He chuffed and rubbed his cheek on my arm, which reminded me of something a dog would do and melted my heart. I patted the top of his head. Once you've ridden your polar bear familiar through the frozen Alaskan tundra at night, you're not afraid to pet him anymore. At least, I wasn't, and I couldn't imagine who would be.

I surveyed Lloyd's house. It was a hodgepodge of mismatched materials, with metal pieces nailed on to replace boards in some sections, a tarp draped over half the roof, and metal rods zip-tied on to replace the porch step railings. The place was dark. But light spilled out of a nearby house, which I knew was Carla Swanson's. I didn't care to be seen, so I gestured for Ragnar to follow me around back.

Picking our way along the side of the house to the back was an exercise in patience—debris was scattered everywhere, poking out of deep snow. It looked like trash, building materials, and stuff that was flat-out unidentifiable.

I thought of Carla and how she'd openly said she hated Lloyd. Did she get so tired of his mess and how he had disrespected her property that she hit him in the head with her walking stick?

I thought it was certainly possible.

We had to forge a path through the junk in the deep snow by tapping carefully with our feet as we went—I was afraid of stepping on a rusty nail.

As I stepped onto the back porch after we finally made it there, the structure swayed below me, inducing a wave of vertigo. Another step, and the wood beneath my feet sagged as though rotten.

This place was a fire trap wrapped in a safety hazard.

The back door wouldn't budge. Lloyd probably had it secured by at least a deadbolt or two, knowing his propensity for believing in imminent disaster by alien invasion.

I stepped back and considered my limited options. The only thing I could come up with to try was somehow getting the door open with magic. Another vision of the ice glacier I'd created back at Grandpa's store and how Ragnar had to save me danced in my brain. Would I never get over that enough to try more magic?

But I also didn't want to embarrass myself again.

Step back.

I did as my polar bear familiar telepathically ordered me, pushing aside how very weird that was. What was he planning to do? It wasn't a long wait to find out.

Ragnar started in the yard and took a running leap onto the porch and charged straight at the door. I covered my eyes at the last second as he rammed his shoulder into the wood, so I didn't see the impact, but the thundering thud, splintering wood, and screeching metal noises made it clear what had happened.

I peered between my fingers at the smashed-up door hanging from one hinge.

"Thanks," I muttered. So much for not drawing Carla's attention. Unless she listened to the TV as loud as Grandpa did, there was no way she wouldn't have heard that cacophony in the quiet.

So I'd better hurry.

I took a careful step over the wreckage into the house but stopped immediately when a stench like none I'd ever encountered hit me like a physical wall. I gagged and shoved my face deeper into the parka. "What is that?" I choked out.

Ragnar growled. *I'm not going in there. Shout if something attacks you. If it does, do your best to lead them out here so I can eat them. I don't want to dine in such conditions.*

I chuckled but regretted it when I had to breathe deeper as a result. "Is it a dead body?" Not wanting to flip on the light and draw Carla's attention if she wasn't already headed over with a shotgun, I waited for my eyes to adjust. I could already tell the place was a wreck. Stacks of stuff was piled to the ceiling everywhere I looked, leaving only narrow walkways.

When my vision had adjusted as much as I expected it to, I inched forward. *If I find a body in here, I'm going to die.*

You will not. You didn't die when you found Lloyd.

That was true. But somehow, in this hoarder's home, it seemed like it would be far creepier to stumble upon a corpse.

Claustrophobia mixed with the clingy, rotten odor made my heart rate click up. I couldn't even do deep breathing to slow it—I'd probably pass out if I tried. I picked up the pace, brushing past stacks of newspapers, old magazines, and empty food tins. The cans hadn't been cleaned well if at all, so I felt better that the stench was probably not a body.

One section of boxes looked new. I stopped and peeked into one of them. A bunch of knives.

What the...

I checked the next stack. Bungie cords.

As I opened more boxes, I found more supplies. Boots in various sizes. Sunglasses meant for walking on the tundra in bright light to avoid snow blindness. Fishing line.

I realized I was looking at the supplies Dawes had bought to resell through his prepper website. There was nothing here that was any different from what we sold in the store, even though he'd been telling folks his stuff was better.

Including the fishing line.

I rolled my eyes and moved on, unwilling to spend more time with the terrible odor than I had to.

Relief hit me when I emerged from the stacks of junk into a slightly clearer space with a small desk, an overflowing trash can, and a bookshelf sagging with tomes. I pulled out my cell phone and turned on the flashlight, confident the light wouldn't be seen through the windows from this deep in the house.

I swept the light over the shelves. Mostly prepper guides and books with titles that foretold varying doomsday scenarios. A few were dystopian novels I had a feeling Lloyd may have treated like non-fiction.

I turned the light onto the desk, where a calendar sat open to the current month, a red pen resting on its face. I leaned closer to read the entries. Lloyd's handwriting was chicken scratch, but it was rapidly apparent that the majority of the entries were prepper meetings in Cross Creek, the next town over from Frost Peak. At the top of the calendar, red ink encircled a number and the word Phil.

That must be Phil Albertson, the leader of the local prepper group. I remembered Nina telling me her ex-boyfriend, Phil, didn't like Lloyd and wanted him out of the group.

There was a red circle around the day Lloyd died. There had been a meeting earlier that day.

Could Phil have finally had enough of Lloyd that day?

I punched the encircled number into my phone's contacts and retraced my steps through the house, hurrying off the porch and into the yard before removing my face from the parka and dragging in deep breaths of fresh air.

No body? Ragnar's tone was bored.

Nope. Just a lot of junk. Lloyd's main hangout was the local prepper group meetings.

Ragnar bobbed his massive head, then sat so I could scramble onto his back again. In an instant, he was loping away from Lloyd's depressing house and back toward town.

I laid my face on his neck and enjoyed the ride. It wasn't at all jerky but smooth and comfortable. As we traveled, I thought about what

I'd seen. Lloyd Dawes' life had been distilled into a stinky house piled with junk and little else.

What would happen to the house? To all the stuff? Lloyd's poor sister would probably have to go through it and figure out what to do with everything. Or maybe Mickey Grimes would take a torch to the whole place and start over.

Melancholy settled on my shoulders, seeming to drive me closer to Ragnar. How sad to think about your life being over and people only remembering you for your eccentricities and annoying tendencies.

For your stinky house full of junk.

I couldn't let my life end without more than that. Some kind of meaning—something left behind besides my clothes and a bunch of scribbled drawings on scraps of paper.

My magical ability. Maybe I could make a mark for good in the world with it. It was worth a try, anyway. But I needed to train and learn as much as I could about how to control it. Become the best witch I could be and use magic to help people. I remembered thinking something similar after I moved the shoe box in Grandpa's store. I'd been right then, and coming to the same conclusion now made me feel better, just in time for Ragnar to slow to a stop in front of Grandpa's store. I slid off, already getting better at the whole polar bear riding thing.

But he stayed seated after I dismounted, staring at the sky above the mountain range. I followed his gaze and drew in a sharp breath.

Green and white lights danced across the sky, making me think of a native dance I'd seen once when I visited my grandparents—all grace and rhythm and light.

I put an arm around Ragnar's shoulders. "It's magnificent."

This is where you need to be. This place is in your soul. You just have to open your heart to it completely. Your life is meaningful and important.

I blinked in surprise at his words, wondering for a moment if he'd somehow heard my thoughts on the ride, but I quickly realized he was right. I had been holding a piece of myself back from diving into life in Frost Peak entirely. I'd been retaining the thought that I could always go back to California. I started to tell him I'd love to commit completely, but everyone in this town thought I was a murderer.

But I didn't want to be argumentative. He'd helped me so much. Instead, I said, *I'm sorry I don't have any gummy bears handy to give you. If you wait here, I'll run inside and grab you a bag.*

But faintly, from inside the store, I heard Grandpa call my name.

Get out of here! I made a shooing motion at Ragnar, not wanting my grandfather to see him. *And thanks for tonight. I'll owe you the gummy bears.*

He chuffed and loped away, disappearing into the darkness. I took one last look at the aurora before heading inside, more sure than ever about the need to find Lloyd's real killer so I could settle down and focus on my new life in this amazing place.

Chapter 9

The next morning, I was out of the store early, determined and on a mission. Having seen Lloyd's house, I knew that Mickey Grimes had motive to kill his renter. After all, Lloyd had absolutely trashed the place. If Aput was right and Mickey wanted to build a hotel there, it would take a bunch of work before he could do it, and with Lloyd occupying the house, it would be even longer.

Plus, Carla had said the landlord for sure wanted Lloyd out, even asking her for help accomplishing it.

The internet had easily delivered Mickey's office address. As I walked across town toward it, I used voice-to-text to send a message to Nina, asking if she'd help me retrieve the dead snowmobile later. Hopefully, Grandpa or Aput wouldn't notice it was gone before I could get it tucked back in the shed.

Mickey's office building was a single story with lots of windows. I entered an airy lobby with a ton of natural light, which was good because it wasn't too large.

The receptionist used an intercom to announce my visit to Mickey. He told her he'd see me. She led me down a couple of hallways, past conference rooms and other offices, to drop me in a big office at the end of a wide corridor.

Mickey sat behind a metal and glass desk and eyed me with his head tilted. "I'm surprised to see you here."

He didn't invite me to sit, so I stood awkwardly. The room was decorated with pictures of buildings. I assumed they were Mickey's developments, though some were in much bigger cities than you'd find anywhere in Alaska.

A coat rack stood to my right, with a beige parka hanging on it and a pair of heavy winter boots next to it.

I pushed my parka's hood back. "Yeah, to be honest, I was nervous coming here after what happened at the community center yesterday. I mean, I can totally understand why Molly Dawes is lashing out. She lost her brother. But, anyway, I wanted to stop by and clear the air between us. I'm new here, and I don't want any hard feelings with other business owners or anything."

He made a noise like a clearing of the throat, but the way he snickered at the same time told me it was a weird form of laugh. "That's awfully big of you. To offer an olive branch to your competition like this."

"Competition? What do you mean?" My hands felt clammy, so I pulled off the mittens as uneasiness stirred in my belly.

The smirk deepened. "I'm opening a bigger, better store than Spitzer's soon. In Cross Creek." He leaned back and opened his arms. "I expect to attract a lot of business since I plan to have things in stock at all times that George can't seem to keep on the shelves."

At least a dozen thoughts ran through my mind. I'd already heard this rumor, but here it was right from the guy's own lips. The vague insult toward my grandfather had my anger flaring, but it was quickly overwhelmed by a stab of nerves.

I worked on keeping my expression placid, even though I didn't feel that way. If Mickey Grimes opened a new store, people might be even more likely to go there if they thought I was a murderer.

I had to figure out who had killed Lloyd and clear my name.

Too much time had passed since Mickey spoke while I stood blinking and thinking. I had to say something. I stammered, "That sounds like quite an endeavor. We wish you well—I'm sure there's room for two stores here." I wasn't sure of that at all. It wasn't like the population was booming in this neck of the woods.

He made the weird laugh sound again. "We'll see. So that's the only reason you're here? To clear the air?" He made finger quotes as he said the last three words and, boy, was that irritating. The guy was so smug it was all I could do to stand there and speak civilly to him. I wanted to tell him off good.

But my nerves fluttered. I didn't want Mickey to figure out I was there sniffing around to find clues about whether he killed Lloyd. If that dawned on him, I could be in trouble. After all, this guy could very well be a murderer. I couldn't put it past him to attack again if he thought someone was close to catching him.

But I also didn't want to leave without at least trying to get some information.

I nodded. "That and I'm slowly making the rounds, getting to know people and other business owners here. So, hi!" What a ridiculous thing to say. I had to stop myself from slapping my own forehead at what an idiot I was.

Okay. No more foolishness. It was time to get down to business. I steeled my nerves and jumped in. "You know, someone told me you were Lloyd's landlord. I happened to drive by his place yesterday with my friend Nina. She was showing me the lay of the land around here. Dawes' yard and house sure were a mess."

His mouth twisted in disgust. "He was a hoarder, a slob, and a nut about his doomsday ridiculousness. I'm glad I don't have to deal with him anymore. Do you know how hard it is to legally get someone out of your property when you rent it out?" He shook his head. "It's un-American, if you ask me. I should be able to kick anyone out at any time for any reason. I mean, I can, I guess, but actually getting them out physically is another story. That takes lawyers and cops—not a cop like we have here. That sheriff is useless. Here, it takes some thinking outside the box to liberate your property from what amounts to a filthy squatter, that's for sure."

Thinking outside the box. Like murdering the occupant to get your property back? Surely, that could be considered outside the box. But if Aput was right about Mickey's history, would doing something like that really be very far out of his wheelhouse?

"What are your plans for the place now?"

"First I have to get everything out of there. That'll take a pretty penny —hiring someone to empty it. Heaven knows I'm not going in there myself. I think it's probably filled with biohazards."

I fought back a shudder, thinking of how I'd touched stuff in that house. What *was* that smell anyway? I forced myself to let it go and refocus on the guy speaking in front of me.

"Then I'm going to tear the place down and put up a quaint little hotel. Only ten rooms or so. Maybe eight. Maybe twelve. Give Bob Dearing a little competition." He barked a laugh that didn't sound mirthful. "Anyway, I'll make a killing on it in the summer. Everybody wants to feel like a local in a remote Alaskan village for four to seven days. Plus, it's closer to Cross Creek than Frost Peak, so the folks who rent there will need to stock up on supplies at my new store. I have a few other properties around both Frost Peak and Cross Creek to convert to short-term rentals too. Your grandfather should start looking for another source of income." His expression couldn't be more smug. Once again, I wished for the ability to put him in his place instead of catering to him, pretending to be nice.

The receptionist's voice came through Mickey's speaker, asking him to take a call. He held up a finger to me and grabbed his phone. He spun his chair halfway around, away from me.

I stood there, feeling awkward. Maybe I should slip out while he was talking?

I looked around again. The parka caught my attention. Particularly the buttons. My eyes nearly popped out when I realized they were the same as the one I'd found near Lloyd's body. At least I thought they were—the jacket was a little too far away for me to see whether they had the herringbone pattern. But they sure looked the same from where I stood.

I squinted. Were there any buttons missing? The top two and bottom one were there, but at least a couple in the middle weren't visible due to the tuck of the fabric.

Biting back a groan of frustration, I wished I could use magic to help me. Like, maybe I could freeze Mickey long enough to run over and check the remaining few buttons.

But I knew I couldn't do that and almost groaned again. What good was being a witch if you couldn't even use your power to help solve a murder?

Mickey hung up the phone and twirled to face me. "I have a meeting in a few minutes, so I'll have to cut this air-clearing-fest short."

His sarcasm made me want to jab back with some snark of my own, but I forced a smile. "I'll be on my way, then."

He nodded and pulled a file out of a drawer. His voice stopped me in the doorway. "If I were you, I'd make sure that grandfather of yours was set up in a nice home or something. My new store will probably run him out of business, and with you in jail for murder, he won't have anyone to take care of him."

I ground my teeth and headed forward without answering.

Wow, this guy was a major jerk. But was he a murderer? He was definitely high on my list, but I hadn't gained any proof, that was for sure.

As I shuffled down the hall, I felt down. I hadn't gained any information in that discussion—except the troubling fact that Mickey was opening a competing store. But I was no closer to proving someone besides me had killed Lloyd.

I breathed a heavy sigh, my shoulders feeling heavy. The perpetual darkness was starting to weigh me down too. Maybe I should use one of the happy lights Grandpa sold. I could set it up in my room upstairs and sit under it for a while every day. Lots of the residents of Frost Peak swore by them, including Nina.

Ahead of me, a cleaning person with a cart came out of an office. I focused on her and recognized Molly Dawes.

And if she wasn't the last person I wanted to run into, I didn't know who was. I didn't need another round of accusations thrown at me. I made an abrupt turn to head down an adjoining hallway and quickened my steps. After a few wrong turns, I found an exit door and stepped outside, glad to have gotten around Molly.

The airport lay in front of me, though it was a decent walk away. I stood for a second, unsure.

My mom hadn't wanted me to know about magic. She'd thought it would make my life harder. I'd been giving that some thought off and on since my first impromptu lesson at the store with Nina and Grandpa. I'd wondered if I should honor what she thought and keep my non-magical life intact. Maybe things would be harder for me if I was a witch on top of everything else.

But was Mom right? I mean, sure there may be some aspects of my life that would be easier without magic. But wasn't it denying my true potential? It was like finding out my parents were Olympic athletes but never trying out sports myself because they had injuries at the ends of their careers and didn't want me to have the same experience.

My experience may not be the same as Mom's. I wanted to live my best life—embrace everything it had to offer me.

Then I thought about my ex. Chad had left me virtually at the altar and was part of the reason I was in Frost Peak. I imagined his face if he could see me doing magic, after he'd basically told me I was too boring for him to make a life with.

A smile broke over my face.

I headed for the airport.

Chapter 10

Nina cocked a hip and crossed her arms. "You went by yourself, didn't you?"

I widened my eyes in innocence but didn't answer.

"You did. What happened?"

Maybe I could distract her from this line of questioning. I chewed my lip.

Nina pinned me with an even look. She wasn't going to give up. I blew out a breath. "The snowmobile ran out of gas, and the radio battery died."

Her expression didn't change for so long, I wondered if she'd heard. But we were in a hangar with no one else around. It was echoey. She'd probably heard me twice.

Finally, Nina groaned and rubbed her temple. "How'd you get back? And where's the snowmobile now?"

"I walked. Partway. Then I rode Ragnar. The snowmobile is still out there. That was the second thing I was going to talk to you about."

"Rode . . . Back up, Cali-girl. What's a Ragnar?"

Oh. Right. She didn't know about that.

"He's my familiar. The polar bear we saw in the distance the day I got here." I eyed her, wondering how she'd react.

Erupting into belly laughter wasn't what I expected. She laughed so hard, she doubled over and shoved a fist into her side.

It was my turn to cross my arms. I watched her guffaws with a frown. She gasped dramatically for air and tried to straighten. Then the giggles took over again, and tears streamed. She held up a finger. "Sorry," she gasped.

I sat on a metal bench and studied my fingernails while she tried to gain control of herself. Eventually, she wiped her eyes, and the gales trickled to snickers. I arched a brow at her.

"Sorry," she said again. "I can't believe you have a polar bear familiar."

That made me think of something I hadn't before. "Do you have a familiar?"

She nodded. "A ferret. He doesn't like the cold and stays home wrapped in a blanket inside a cat bed most of the time. He's not particularly helpful, and he eats way more than you'd ever expect a two-pound animal to eat."

I was glad I didn't have to feed Ragnar. The thought of how much he'd need to eat and what his diet consisted of made me queasy. "Okay, if you're done laughing at me now..."

She shook her head. "I wasn't laughing *at* you. But the idea of you riding a magical polar bear through the dark tundra punched me right in the funny bone. I'll stop, I promise. And we'll get your snowmobile home." She headed across the hangar. "There are some extra gas cans around here. We can go on my snowmobile."

"Hold on."

She offered me a curious look.

"Thanks, and I will take you up on that, but first, I want to ask you something."

"Shoot." She ran her hands through her hair, working on tangles as she went.

"Can you give me a magic lesson?"

"Right now?" Nina's brow wrinkled. "It's daytime."

"I know. But I don't know how to do anything. Last night, there was zero I could do to keep myself alive and safe except to start trekking across the snow and praying I wouldn't freeze to death before I got to town. I don't like that feeling. If I'm a witch, I want to be able to act like one." I didn't add that I wanted to be able to freeze people so I could look for evidence in the murder investigation I was up to my eyebrows in. I was pretty sure she wouldn't like that reason.

Her expression softened. "That makes sense. I was hoping to do all the lessons with your granddad around. I don't want him accusing me of teaching you wrong or something."

"He won't be able to have a lesson until after work today. I'd like to learn at least something small right now." I hesitated and then winced. "Actually, I did try some magic after you taught me how to move the shoebox."

"With your granddad?"

I shook my head. "Alone." I told her about the glacier I'd somehow created while trying to clean the walkway behind the store. "That's when I met Ragnar for the first time. He showed up and made the glacier go away."

Nina's jaw dropped. "He did magic?"

"Yeah. He said he has some power to help me when I need it." He hadn't used it against the wolves, though. That rescue had been accomplished with pure brute force.

She whistled low. "Wow. Stardust—my ferret—doesn't do anything magical. He only prattles on to me telepathically in a lecturey voice anytime I'm within twenty feet of him. Then he demands food." Nina pulled a face. "I wonder why you got a magical familiar."

I shrugged. She knew more about being a witch than I did. If she didn't know, I sure didn't. But it made me wonder if Timber had magical ability.

"Okay," Nina said. "I'll give you a little lesson. Hopefully, your granddad won't kill me for it." She took off her parka—which I hoped I didn't have to do because, while the hangar wasn't as cold as being outside, it also wasn't toasty—and pushed back her long sleeves. "Okay, let's talk about control. When you're getting ready to cast a spell, you need to have the clearest vision of the results you want as possible already set up in your mind."

I nodded, thoughtful. Maybe that's what I'd done wrong with the clean-up outside the store. I'd wanted to get the mess to go away, but I didn't have a clear idea of how that should happen. I'd simply wanted it to be clean and figured the magic would figure out the how of it.

"So, let's practice doing that." Nina looked around until her eyes lit on a broom and mop leaning on the wall. "Okay, watch this." She focused on the items, her lips moved, and she performed a complicated flourish with her wrist. The broom jumped to attention. She did another flourish, and it started working on the floor, sweeping dust into a neat little pile. A third flourish, and it returned to rest next to the mop.

She looked at me and smiled brightly. "So I envisioned the process— what it would look like for the broom to sweep that area of the floor. Then, I kind of directed it to happen. Easy peasy, Cali-girl. You try."

I bit my lower lip, trying not to visualize the glacier I'd created before. Thinking about something going wrong was almost certainly not a good way to go. I shook out my wrists and bounced on the balls of my feet.

Nina grinned in amusement but said nothing.

"Okay." I thought about what I wanted to happen—the broom becoming animated and sweeping the section next to the one Nina had done. I thought about how I had made the box of shoes move the first time I tried magic in the store. I *could* do this. I was a witch. All I needed to do was focus hard.

I envisioned the desired effect again, this time putting myself in the moment as firmly as possible. I thought about the sound of the broom bristles on the concrete floor and imagined the tiny puff of dust coming off them as they moved. My nose twitched as I thought of getting a little errant powder into it as the broom kicked it up.

Feeling great about the detailed picture in my mind, I breathed out a rhyme. "Dirt and grime, you're out of time." I flicked my wrist—with a not-so-eloquent flourish as Nina's—and pushed intention into it.

The broom handle twitched. Then the whole broom moved. It danced around the section next to the one Nina had done, sweeping dust into a pile.

It was working. I broke into a wide smile and looked to Nina for approval. But a wrinkle appeared between her eyebrows, and her lips quirked as she watched the clean-up.

I glanced back. It swept faster. Dust rose into the air in a dark cloud. The broom skipped its way through the pile Nina had already gathered, kicking up even more dirt. A mini tornado of swirly dust meandered through the air. It seemed to hover for a moment. Then it headed directly for my nose. I threw my hands over my face, batting at the cloud. But it was too late.

A massive sneeze erupted, followed by half a dozen small ones. The dust tornado fell to the ground, followed by the broom, suddenly inert.

My eyes watered, and I rubbed my nose vigorously. A coughing fit attacked me next. My throat felt like fire had laced its way down it— swollen and raw.

By the time I could breathe again and my eyes had stopped watering, Nina had picked up the broom and returned it to its spot. She stood observing me.

I groaned. "I'm sorry."

She shook her head and handed me a bottle of water I hadn't seen before.

"I think I over-visualized." I coughed again and then gulped cool water before adding, "Is that a thing?"

She lifted a shoulder and let it fall. "I guess. Never happened to me though." As soon as the words were out of her mouth, she winced and hurried over to me. "I'm sorry. I didn't mean that. It's not you. I'm probably a terrible teacher."

"How did you learn?"

"Oh, hmm. I don't remember actually being taught a lot of this stuff. Remember, I always knew I was a witch, from my earliest memory. I think learning magic for many people is sort of like learning to talk or walk. You don't necessarily remember the mechanics of how you learned it—it just happened during everyday life."

"That makes sense." I felt a stab of annoyance at my mom for keeping my gift a secret from me and actually spelling me to keep me from learning, but I sighed and pushed it away. It couldn't be changed now. "Thanks for trying."

"You sound like the lesson's over. Don't you want to try again?"

I cut my eyes to her face. She smiled.

"You're still willing to try? Even though I made a mess of things?"

She threw her hands up. "I'm a glutton for punishment. Let's back up and try something even simpler. I probably rushed you into too complicated of a maneuver."

I wasn't so sure. Maybe magic wasn't my forte. Perhaps you had to learn it along with every other life skill mastered in toddlerhood to be proficient at it. Magic and using a potty—hand-in-hand abilities.

But I said nothing. Nina was sweet to try, and I was willing to give it another shot.

Nina paced around a bit, deep in thought. Then she brightened. "One of the first things most witches do with magic as babies is telekinesis."

"Like we did with the shoebox?"

"Yes! They call something to them that they want. It makes it even harder for witch moms to deal with their kids than it is for human moms. They can't put something out of reach and expect it to stay there." She hooted out a laugh. "When I was a baby, my mom couldn't have any butter in the house because I'd call it to me and eat it plain until I was sick." She winced. "Now, I can't eat butter at all."

The thought of summoning something to me sounded better than working with the broom. After all, I'd already done it, to a small degree, with the shoebox, so I knew it was at least possible. "Okay. What do I do?"

"Let's use this." Nina set a sponge on the seat of a nearby metal chair. "Okay, so you fill your mind with the idea that you must have the sponge. There's no other option than for it to come to you. It simply must be in your hand." She paused, pursing her lips. "Actually, I think that's it. Imagine it in your hand, not moving from the chair *to* your hand." She nodded. "Yeah, I think that's it."

"Do I need a rhyme?"

"Since this is so basic, let's try without. Maybe that's tripping you up a bit. Instead, do the visualization and use your intention only. Go ahead whenever you're ready."

I noticed she stepped several feet away from both the sponge and me and figured she had chosen a sponge for a reason. It wouldn't hurt anyone if it beaned them in the head.

"Okay." I focused on emptying my mind of everything but the sponge across the room. I thought about how much I needed it. Imagined it sitting nicely in my hand instead of over there on the cold chair where it wasn't doing anyone any good.

From the corner of my eye, I caught Nina's slight nod. She must have approved of my focus.

But noticing that wasn't keeping my concentration on the sponge, so I blocked Nina out and redoubled my effort. Once I thought I had the image of the sponge sharp enough in my mind, I raised a hand, gave a flourish, and poured my intention into the spell. Then I held out my palm to catch the sponge.

The sponge twitched. I thought that might be all it would do. I pushed more intention toward the idea of the sponge in my hand. It sat up, looking like nothing so much as a prairie dog on high alert. Then it zoomed toward me. My eyes widened. It was heading for my face. Then it was on me, bouncing off my nose, forehead, eyes, and lips. It dove into my neck crease, tickling so much I doubled over. "Stop!" I gasped.

But it wasn't done. It revisited every area of my face again. It acted like an obnoxious puppy, licking me up and down. I batted at it, trying to get it off me, but flailed wildly a few times before I connected. The sponge dove for the ground and hit at the exact instant the hangar door opened.

Sheriff Brodie walked in.

Chapter 11

I gulped and wondered frantically whether Brodie had seen the sponge attack me from the windows in the hangar. A furtive glance at Nina told me she was afraid of the same thing. Her face was a couple shades paler than usual, at least, and she was uncharacteristically amiable. Usually, she would have made an offensive jab at her ex by now.

Brodie shook snow off his parka and stomped his boots. "There you are. Your grandfather suggested you may be here hanging out with Nina."

"Oh." How could Grandpa have possibly known that? I hadn't intended to visit Nina at all when I left the shop earlier. Was it witch magic he used or just the magic of a grandfather who was fond of his granddaughter? "So you found me. What's up?"

He looked around, and his gaze dropped to the sponge on the floor. But his eyes popped up again, and his expression didn't change. I relaxed a fraction. Seemed as though we'd dodged a close call on that one, and the sheriff hadn't seen us doing magic.

"I got back to town a few hours ago."

"You weren't gone as long as you thought."

He nodded. "Weather held up, and things went smoothly. I hurried back to dig into the Lloyd Dawes case."

The Lloyd Dawes case. There it was again—a man's life reduced to almost nothing. A case name and a bunch of junk in a run-down old house. "Any leads?"

His eyes darted to Nina.

"Oh, you only want to talk to *one* lay person about your homicide case. Not two. I totally get it." Nina's snark was back full-force, so she must have come to the same conclusion that he hadn't seen anything. She headed for the door.

Brodie rolled his eyes but didn't engage. When Nina was gone, he said, "Someone left an anonymous tip on my office voicemail about the murder."

"Really?" I leaned forward, eager to hear something that might help crack the case. "What was it?"

"That the object used to kill Lloyd may have been the fire poker from your grandfather's store. I confiscated it to send to Anchorage. They'll check it for DNA. Did you hit Lloyd over the head with a fire poker, Frankie?"

"Of course not," I snapped. "I did shake it at him a few times, trying to encourage him to return the items he shoplifted from my grandfather." I crossed my arms. "We need that poker, by the way. When will we get it back?"

His eyebrows drew together until he resembled a comically confused cartoon character. "Never," he said slowly.

I stomped my foot. "How are we supposed to get the logs in the right place in the wood stove?"

"You run a supply store. Can't you take a new poker off the shelf?"

"Sure, if we want to eat into our bottom line." I scowled. "The police department should reimburse us for stealing it."

"Yeah, that isn't going to happen." He chuckled.

The sound of his laughter made me want to explode. I fisted my hands and started to tell him how arrogant and exasperating he was.

But at the last second, I stopped myself, only letting out a muffled gurgle.

"What?"

I shook my head. "Nothing. I didn't hit Dawes with a fire poker or anything else. But I do have a couple ideas about leads you may want to pursue."

He tipped his head and looked at me like an indulgent parent might look at a child telling a story about their invisible friend. "Who's that?"

It took a mighty effort to keep from telling him right off. Instead, I ignored his condescending tone and said, "Phil Albertson and Mickey Grimes. Have you considered them yet?"

His expression morphed into thoughtfulness. "No."

"Grimes wanted Lloyd out of the property he rented. Wants to turn it into a small hotel. Which, by the way, I think is kind of weird because there will be at least half a year where it will mostly sit empty, but he's convinced it'll make a killing. Along with the new store in Cross Creek, which, don't even get me started on that." I took a breath—I was babbling. "Anyway, that's Mickey's motive. Phil's is that Lloyd was a huge pain in his behind."

He barked out a laugh. "I don't think that's a motive for murder."

I shrugged. "Crime of passion maybe. If someone's a big enough annoyance, another person can snap and kill them without planning to, right?"

"I suppose."

I eyed him. "So are you going to check them out?"

"I'll look into it."

"That's a non-answer. It's a yes or no question." I hesitated, not sure if I should ask the next thing. But then I threw caution to the wind and blurted out, "Can I be involved in the investigation?" Before he could shoot me down, I hurried to explain. "You don't have enough help, right? I could help. Look, I just delivered two suspects to you on a platter. Wasn't that helpful?"

"I admit you've given me something to think about but..."

"But I'm a suspect, so I can't help you investigate, right?" I waved a hand. "Right. I was being silly. Forget I asked."

"How about this..."

Wait, he's going to make me an offer? I couldn't believe I may get to help with the investigation, for real.

"I'll keep you in the loop ... if you'll have dinner with me." He grinned, so adorable I could eat him up.

But wait. What in the world? How had he managed to flip my attitude toward him from exasperation to attraction in half a second?

Still, I wanted to jump on his offer. *Yes! I'd love to have dinner with you. You don't even need to keep me in the loop. Keep me in the dark if you want.*

Er. No. That was not appropriate.

Too much time had gone by since anyone had said anything. "Dinner?" I squeaked. *Brilliant, Frankie.*

He bobbed his head. "At my place." He held up his hands. "Now, I'm not a great cook or anything, but there are a few things I make well. Halibut. Spaghetti. Sometimes burgers on the grill, but that's hit or miss and it's not the right season."

"Oh. Um." I wanted to have dinner with him. I also wanted to be in the know about the murder investigation, mainly to be sure I stayed off the main suspect list. Or got off the main suspect list, since I was surely still on it. So what was there to think about? "Yes. I mean, I'd love to. Thanks. But can we have the spaghetti? I'm getting tired of fish already."

He broke into a wide grin. "You got it. Tomorrow night at five." He told me his address and turned to go.

"Thanks, Sheriff."

He pointed a gloved finger at me. "Call me Jason."

I stood there after he left, alone in the hangar, wondering how in the world I'd managed to land a date with the hottest guy I'd seen in Frost Peak. Hopefully, Nina wouldn't mind me going out with her ex.

And hopefully, I could keep my mind on Lloyd Dawes' case while I was at the gorgeous sheriff's house.

I stood in front of Jason's house. Light spilled through the big window onto the snow pile in the front yard. Jason moved around farther back in the house. I hesitated before knocking on the door. Should I do this?

Grandpa hadn't been completely thrilled when I told him about it. "Are you sure that's a good idea, girl?" he'd asked, scratching his chin and making his beard wobble.

"No. But I like spaghetti. A lot."

"Is he going to make it with real pasta?" Nina had been there too. She hadn't acted upset at all about me dating her ex-boyfriend, but she'd been uber curious about the menu. "'Cuz I haven't had real pasta since I moved up here."

"Too hard to get?" I tried to recall if we had it on the shelves.

"No, I'm on a low carb thing. I don't want to slim my curves, you know. Just keep my muscles tight. But I miss pasta."

"I didn't ask him what kind of noodles he planned to use," I confessed. The last thing on my mind had been the type of pasta the man would prepare. I couldn't stop thinking about his strong jawline and adorable smile. The thought of being alone with him in a social setting had my stomach dancing a tango.

As though in response to the memory, a herd of hummingbirds trounced through my gut again. Hopefully, it would settle down enough for me to enjoy whatever kind of pasta Jason made.

I started forward, but a sound made me stop and listen. It was quite distant, but I recognized it. A roar.

Ragnar.

How could I be sure it was my polar bear? I couldn't. Also, since when did I consider him mine?

Since he let me ride him, I supposed.

But still, the nerves in my belly settled after I heard him, and I felt calmer as I continued to the front door knowing my familiar had my back.

Jason Brodie beamed when he opened the door. He swept an arm, inviting me in.

When you live in the tundra, both getting geared up to go outside and getting everything off once you were there was a process that took more than a trivial amount of time. And when a gorgeous guy is standing there watching you get your boots, parka, and mittens off, it feels like it takes a year.

Brodie took my coat and hung it on the rack next to his. Then he opened a closet door, pulled out a pair of soft moccasins, and dropped them by my feet. They matched the ones he wore but were smaller. In response to my questioning look, he said, "I keep them around for when my sister visits."

I slipped them on and groaned. "They're so comfortable." I followed him into the living room and was pleasantly surprised by the décor. It didn't feel like a bachelor pad but was warm, cozy, and neat. A fire sparkled in a brick fireplace facing a plaid-upholstered love seat. The coffee table held magazines on fishing and men's health. The walls, painted light brown, were dotted with framed photos of Alaskan scenery and wildlife.

"Your place is nice."

"Thanks. I like it to be as relaxing as possible for when I'm here."

I followed him into the kitchen. The appliances were dated, with white plastic surfaces, and the countertops were cream-colored laminate with a few ringed stains. But it was clean. "Look at that coffee maker!" It was so fancy, I doubted I could use it without a primer.

He ducked his head. "I splurged on it. I like drinking coffee all day—I start with caffeine and end with decaf. So, I get my money's worth out of it."

I wandered to the stove and lifted the lid off a pot. Red sauce bubbled happily inside. Closing my eyes, I inhaled deeply. "This smells amazing."

"My grandmother's recipe. It's never failed me." He slipped on an oven mitt and pulled a tray of garlic bread out onto the counter.

My stomach growled. "I can't wait to dig in."

He retrieved a bowl of salad from the fridge and then made quick work of putting pasta, sauce, and garlic bread into serving bowls. "Grab that bottle of wine, will you?"

"Sure." The Merlot was airing on the end of the counter, and I snagged it along with the two glasses Jason had set out next to it. The round dining table was tucked into a corner of the kitchen and barely large enough to hold everything plus two plates and the set of candles flickering in its center. "This looks lovely." I ignored the chips on the light blue plates and smiled at him.

He pulled out a chair and waved a hand. "Have a seat."

"Thank you." He reminded me of a kid, proud to show off his schoolwork to a doting parent.

He sat across from me and poured wine for both of us. "Dig in," he said. "I don't stand on ceremony, so help yourself, and don't be shy. Elbows on the table are a-okay with me."

"I'm never shy when food is involved." I piled my plate high with spaghetti and garlic bread and filled the salad bowl to the brim. The first bite of pasta made it clear the noodles were real. I moaned again. "This is delicious," I said around the bite. I almost blabbed that Nina would be jealous, but at the last second, I remembered they'd dated and swallowed the words. No need to remind him of his ex right now.

He fist-pumped in victory at my reaction and then looked toward the ceiling. "Thanks, Granny." He stuffed a big bite into his mouth and grinned while he chewed.

"Yeah, thanks, Granny," I echoed. "And thank *you*, Jason. It's nice to relax and enjoy a meal that isn't fish."

He chuckled. "I hear you. Other than the cuisine, how are you liking Frost Peak?"

I finished chewing, considering my answer. I swallowed and took a sip of wine before I spoke. "I feel like I'm home, to be honest." It was true, but I'd only realized it that moment. "It's totally weird and makes me sound like a freak, but I think this place has called to me my whole life."

"You grew up in California?"

I nodded. "Mom moved us there when I was around two, so I don't remember living here at all." A thought jolted me. Had my mother moved us to keep me from finding out I was a witch?

It made sense. There were so many folks in Frost Peak with magic—if Mom wanted me to grow up without knowing I had power, staying here would have made it more difficult than moving away. A wash of sadness rolled over me as I thought about how things would have been different if I'd stayed and learned magic from the beginning.

For one thing, I'd have never met Chad. That would have been nice.

I shoved the thoughts away. I'd had a good childhood, and Mom was gone now. I didn't want to waste time being upset with her when she'd done what she thought was best for me.

And my relationship with Chad had taught me what I did want. And what I wanted to avoid. It was good I hadn't missed that experience.

Besides, I was here now. Time to make the best of it. "Yeah. I like it here. I mean, it would be better if I wasn't the prime suspect in a murder, but I guess that's just details, right?" I took a bite of garlic bread. My eyes widened. "Did you make this from scratch?" I covered my mouth to keep crumbs in as I talked with my mouth full.

"Yep. The dough recipe is easy. I didn't churn the butter, though." He winked.

"Well, then, I'm not sure I can be bothered to eat it." I used a fake haughty tone. "Non-pure butter could ruin my palate forever." I put the back of a hand to my forehead like Scarlet O'Hara. Then I dissolved into giggles and took another big bite of bread.

Jason laughed too. "I'll keep that in mind for next time." His eyes shot to mine as he realized what he'd said. "I mean, if there's a next time. I hope there is."

I was glad my mouth was full of bread, so I didn't have to answer. I wanted there to be a next time too, but I wasn't sure it was a good idea. As soon as I swallowed, I changed the subject. "What about you? Are you from Frost Peak?"

He shook his head. "I'm from Anchorage. When this job came up, I was intrigued. I liked the idea of helping a remote town like this. And I was looking to get out of there for other reasons." He didn't meet my eyes. "So I applied and got it."

I spun pasta around my fork. "Do you like it?"

"I love it. I mean, it can be stressful. Especially when there's a lot going on, and I feel like I can't take care of it all at once. But it's also super rewarding. I love the people here. They're full of grit, but most of them are also amazingly kind." He pointed his fork at me. "What about you? Why'd you decide to leave California? I mean, I know your grandpa probably needs help, but picking up and leaving your life is a big deal."

I didn't want to talk about Chad, not only because I was having a nice time and didn't care to think about him, but also because I didn't want it to sound like a sob story. But there was no way to avoid the direct question. "My fiancé changed his mind about getting married. And I decided it would be nice to start over somewhere he doesn't live." I waved a hand, trying to indicate it was no big deal. "A new start is nice sometimes."

He was quiet for a minute, then cleared his throat. "What I mentioned before about having other reasons for leaving Anchorage?"

I nodded.

"It was a similar situation. Except my girlfriend didn't have enough integrity to break up with me outright. Instead, she cheated on me for a few months. Lied to my face." He frowned and looked at his plate.

"I'm sorry."

"Nah, don't be. It's history. I didn't mean to bring it up."

We finished eating, both quiet. Then Jason said, "Do you like board games?"

"Does Santa like black licorice?"

He squinted and cocked his head. "I don't actually know the answer to that."

I grinned. "He does."

He got to his feet and picked up both our plates. "Okay, but wouldn't it make more sense to say eggnog or cookies or something? I never heard a Santa story that included black licorice."

With a shrug, I grabbed the bread and pasta and followed him to the counter. "I guess you'll have to take my word for the fact that he likes it. A lot. So does Rudolph. But the bottom line is I love board games."

He snorted and stuck the plates in the dishwasher. "All right, then. It's not the most exciting after dinner activity in the world, but I have Scrabble, Yahtzee, Monopoly ... basically all the classics. Is there one you prefer?"

"Monopoly, but I doubt you want to play with me. I'm ruthless." I opened drawers until I found plastic wrap, pulled it out, and waved it at him. "Not that I'm more compliant for the other games. Basically, you're going down no matter what we choose to play."

"Huh." He stuck out his jaw. "Big words. How about you put your money where your rather loud mouth is?" He winked to let me know he was joking.

I leaned a hip on the counter. "What're you thinking?"

"Twenty bucks. Winner takes all."

"Hmm." I pushed off the counter and wrapped the bread before answering. "Deal. You choose the game."

He held up both hands. "Hey, if Monopoly's your strongest one, then let's go. I ain't scared." He swaggered to the table with a dishcloth.

When we were finished cleaning up, Jason retrieved the game from a closet. We spent the next hour and a half engrossed in a heated battle that involved me jumping out of my chair several times, Jason tugging on his hair and chewing his bottom lip a lot, and finally, me doing a victory dance that included lots of twirls and stomps.

He handed over the twenty dollars with thin lips. Then he stared into my eyes. "I'm going to want a rematch."

My breath caught. He was close to me. And he had a look I recognized on his face. He wanted to kiss me.

I wanted to kiss him back. But I was a murder suspect, and he was law enforcement. I was also a witch, and he didn't know those existed. At least, I assumed he didn't. And with his history of having been lied to by a woman, I found myself feeling guilty about starting a relationship off on a lie, even if it was one of omission.

"Thank you so much for the fun evening." I stepped back a couple inches.

Jason got the message; he straightened. A flash of disappointment crossed his face, but he covered it with a charming smile. "I had a great time too." He walked me to the door and waited while I got all my stuff on. "Do you want me to walk you home?"

"That's okay. I'll be fine."

He opened the door and waved as I headed out. He watched from the porch until I was well down the sidewalk.

As I walked, enjoying the stillness and quiet, melancholy settled on my shoulders. I wished I could have kissed Jason. But my life was way too complicated for that at the moment. It may be too complicated for a while. After all, I wasn't going to stop being a witch.

But hopefully, I would stop being a murder suspect soon. I squared my shoulders. It was time to stop thinking about romance and start thinking about investigating. Past time.

Chapter 12

"Did you wait up for me, Grandpa? You didn't need to do that." I smiled and sat across the table from him. Our flat was cozy and well-appointed, with comfortable armchairs, worn footstools, and well-loved books. I had my own small room which, so far, didn't have much in the way of my own personal touch. I'd sold most stuff before leaving California and had only the basics shipped to Frost Peak. But I figured I could work on it over time. And, besides, I didn't want to stay with Grandpa forever. It irked me slightly that, as a grown woman, he was providing my room and board. I itched to get out on my own. But I had grabbed a special happy light from inventory and set it up in my room. The lack of sun was wearing on me already.

Grandpa shook his head, setting the long beard to shaking. "I was looking at the books and got caught up in the numbers."

I chuckled. "That'll happen. Numbers are shifty little buggers."

He didn't laugh, which caught my attention as out of character. Instead, the wrinkles in his brow got deeper. "I noticed you moved some inventory around in the books. Took me half an hour to figure out what was what."

"Oh. I'm sorry. I planned to tell you about that tomorrow—I didn't know you'd be looking at it tonight." I reached for the book. "Let me show you my logic."

He snatched the book away, lips thinning. "No. I don't want to see your logic. I want to use the logic I've used for decades. There was nothing wrong with it, and no reason to change it."

My stomach lurched. Grandpa had a quick temper at times. That much I knew. But I hadn't been the recipient of one of his sharp-tongued scoldings before. I didn't like it. Keeping my tone gentle, I tried again. "I think it would help us get a handle on our ordering strategy if we arranged inventory in these families. And maybe we can transfer this information to a computer program. I did some research on good ones and have it narrowed down to a couple. It'll help to have things centralized." I reached for the book again.

He slammed a fist on it, making me jump. "Ordering strategy? Why do we need a new ordering strategy? There's nothing wrong with how I do it. I go through the aisles, see what we're getting low on, and write it down. There's no need to change the books or how we group things or put everything on a dratted computer. The way we do it has been good enough all this time." He rose to his feet and pinned me with a sharp look. "It was good enough for your grandmother." He stalked to his room and closed the door.

My jaw dropped, and guilt stabbed at me. The last thing I wanted to do was upset him or make things harder. That wasn't why I'd come to Frost Peak. If I had to deal with disorderly books, crazy inventory methods, and ineffectual ordering systems, then I would. Should I knock on his door and tell him that?

No. I should let him cool down. It was getting late. I'd talk to him in the morning, when we were both fresh.

I rested my head on my arms and pouted. Mickey Grimes was opening a place in Cross Creek. My grandfather refused to make any tweaks to our ordering system, so we were often out of supplies people wanted and needed.

Worry gnawed at me.

It felt like Spitzer's General Store was under attack from multiple angles. And some of it was friendly fire from my grandfather himself.

"So you're saying it was a good date, right? But you didn't kiss him goodnight?" Fine lines made a funny squiggle across Nina's brow as she gave me an incredulous look.

"That's what I'm saying." I spun a can of beans to face forward on the shelf and moved on to the peaches.

"I won't pretend I'm not baffled by the idea of a good date with Jason to begin with," she mused, following me down the aisle.

"Oh, come on. You didn't have any nice dates with him?"

She shrugged. "I guess. Nothing special, though."

Our date was special. It had been nice, even if it was simple. I even won twenty bucks. "I didn't kiss him because I don't want to lead him on. I have a lot going on right now, and I don't think getting into a relationship is my best bet."

"Because you're a murder suspect? Seems like dating the sheriff might help you with that one." Nina guffawed.

"It's not that alone. It's also the other thing." My eyes darted around, but no one was within ear shot. "The magic thing." I still whispered it, just in case.

"You're going to have to get over that one. Unless you plan to date only wizards. Which I guess you could do, but in a place like Frost Peak, where the man-pond isn't very big to begin with, it gives you even fewer fish to choose from."

"I thought we were talking about guys. Why does everything in this town always come back to fish?" I was already super tired of eating fish. And I only just got here. Not a good sign.

"Sorry. How about this? In a place like Frost Peak, where there are only so many polar bears, you'll have even fewer familiars to choose from."

I gave her a squinty-eyed glare. "Shh." The last thing I needed was for Grandpa to hear us talking about Ragnar, who he had an attitude about. I hadn't seen him yet that morning. I was eager for a chance to smooth things over after our argument the night before. I'd spent most of the night tossing and turning, worrying about how I might have wounded him. I puffed out an enormous sigh.

Nina studied my face. "You're not thinking about Jason anymore, are you?"

"No. I upset Grandpa last night. I feel terrible."

"You should. Didn't anyone ever teach you to respect your elders, Cali-girl?"

I groaned and threw my head back. "I like you and all, but you could learn a thing or two about being supportive."

She chuckled. "I was only joshing about the respect. You have that for your grandfather in spades. Anyone who sees you with him can tell that right away. As for being supportive, the way I give support is by not pulling any punches. I may not be all sunshine and cupcakes, but I'll tell you what I think." She elbowed me gently. "And I hope that's helpful."

"It is. Thanks. But I wish Grandpa would come downstairs, so I can apologize to him."

"He can't stay upstairs forever. He'll run out of food."

I jerked my eyes up to look at her face. "You think he's staying up there on purpose?"

"I don't know. But I can only imagine he's feeling bad about your argument too."

That was a new thought, but she was probably right.

The bells over the door interrupted my thoughts. I looked up to find a young woman with dark, straight hair beaming at me. She opened her arms wide. "Frankie! I can't believe you're finally here."

I studied her for a moment, and then recognition flared in my mind. "Kaia?"

"The one and only."

As I hurried over to embrace my younger cousin, I noticed the pale pink aura around her and mused again about how odd it was that my brain had blocked the memory that she had one from my mind. "It's so good to see you."

"Sorry it took me this long to come welcome you to town." She leaned back in my embrace to study my face. "You look good. The cold air must be agreeing with you."

I glanced at Nina, who laughed like a maniac. "What?" I demanded.

"Nothing. I'm thinking about that jacket you showed up in." To Kaia, she said, "Totally not appropriate for our weather."

Stepping away from my cousin, I crossed my arms. "It was well-researched. Not my fault none of the reviewers tested it in Frost Peak. But don't worry. I'm planning to leave comments about how it's not good for the tundra on all the sites I used when I chose it."

Both of them cracked up at that. When they'd finished laughing, I tried to change the subject. "Do you want some hot tea, Kaia? It's kind of a long trek from the village, isn't it?"

She nodded and took off her parka, heading to the area behind the counter. "It takes about half an hour by sled."

"Sled? You mean, you brought your dog team?" I hurried toward the front window and peered outside. Sure enough, a full-fledged sled was parked right out front, and eight sled dogs curled up in gray, white, and black fuzzy balls in front of it, noses buried in their tails. "Aw! They're so cute."

Kaia rummaged in a cupboard and pulled out a stack of metal bowls. "They need a quick rest and some water before we head back. And I need to pick up supplies for me and some of the other folks who live in my village." She grinned at me. "I volunteered to come fetch stuff so I could say hello to you."

Aput, coming out of an aisle, said, "I'll water the pups. Hi, Kaia."

"Hey!" She handed him the bowls. "Thanks."

He nodded and disappeared into the back room.

Kaia plopped onto a stool and regarded me. "I heard about the drama going on here. With Lloyd Dawes." She shook her head. "I'm actually surprised it took this long for someone to get rid of that twerp."

"You knew him?"

"Everybody knew him. There wasn't anyone he didn't annoy the heck out of. Guy was a real jerk." A scowl darkened her face, and her mouth twisted in a sneer. "Piece of work is what he was, and not a work of art."

"What'd he do to you?" Nina asked, leaning against the counter.

"For one thing, there was his prepper stuff. I told him he should stuff it—he was worrying some of the elders in my village. Making them consider his craziness about aliens or whatever. I thought he was trying to fleece them of what little they have by getting them to think they needed to buy some of his nonsense to survive the coming doom. So I told him where to stick his stories. And I said he needed to stay away from my village's elders." Her eyes seemed to snap and pop like a fire, and she grinned. "He didn't like that a lot."

"I don't imagine so, but it seems like he was fairly used to being told to stay away from people," I ventured.

"Maybe. But he probably wasn't used to what else I called him."

Nina's expression was like a dog with a particularly favorite toy. "Ooh. What did you call him?"

She shook her head. "No way. I'm not going to risk someone hearing me say it. It wasn't nice. But neither was Lloyd. In fact, he treated folks from my village worse than someone may treat a herd of carpenter ants attacking their wooden house."

I squinted. "I don't think that's called a herd..."

Kaia's eyebrows went up, and she glanced at Nina, who gave a long suffering eye roll. "She likes to research things. This isn't the first discussion about herds she's had with herself since arriving here."

"I don't know what it's called exactly," I admitted. "But herd doesn't seem right. I think that may be reserved for animals with hooves."

They both stared at me, silent, until I murmured, "Sorry." I busied myself straightening a display of gum on the counter, so I didn't have to meet their gazes. "So he was, what? A racist?"

Kaia nodded, her expression dark. "Yep. Like I said, I'm surprised it took so long for someone to off him." She got up. "I'd better start my shopping. Once those dogs have rested and eaten, they'll be raring to go. They get obnoxious when they want to run and can't."

"They like pulling the sled all that way?"

"They live for it," Kaia said, love for her dogs evident in her gentle tone. "It's their favorite thing."

I watched her head into the aisles.

"What's that look on your face?" Nina asked.

"What look?"

"You're thinking Kaia's pretty cool all grown up, right?"

I swiped a hand over the counter to sweep off some dust. "Isn't she?"

Nina snorted. "She was born and raised here. Kaia's tough as nails. And her dogs and the good of her village are her world. Lloyd was really taking his life in his hands messing with her friends and family."

I leaned my elbows on the counter and let my head hang. "There are *so* many people who wanted Lloyd dead." I groaned. "How are we supposed to figure out who did it?"

She arched a brow. "We? Are you and Jason working together on the investigation now?"

"No. He said he'd keep me in the loop, though."

Nina's eyes moved to where Kaia had disappeared into the aisle. "Hopefully, his loop narrows soon. I gotta run."

As she left, I chewed on what she'd said. She was right. This investigation needed to tighten up, and fast. There was too much riding on finding the true killer. I chewed my lip as I considered that.

If I didn't clear my name fast, not only could Grandpa's business be negatively affected, but I might also be arrested. Or, even if Jason could clear my name, it might be too late to rescue my reputation in town, resulting in a hostile atmosphere for me here.

I might have to leave Frost Peak.

Chapter 13

After Kaia left and Nina went back to work, I was left swirling in my own thoughts. Grandpa came downstairs but didn't say more than hello to me, and there were too many customers around to discuss our argument with him. It didn't take me long to determine he planned to avoid me, anyway.

Sadness weighed on me as I tried to keep a happy face for folks coming in to buy things. Maybe leaving Frost Peak wouldn't be such a bad thing. Even my grandpa was upset with me, so it wasn't like I was doing a fantastic job being here anyway.

"That's an awfully long face."

I whirled to find Jason Brodie at the end of the plumbing supplies aisle I was working in. "Oh." I forced a smile. "Just thinking, that's all."

"Thinking about Lloyd's case?"

"Among other things."

He jerked his chin behind him. "I can't help with the other stuff, but I'm going to talk to Phil Albertson, and I thought you might want to tag along."

I perked up at that. "Why'd you change your mind? I thought I got to stay in the loop and nothing more." I'd expected only cursory, one-sentence updates on the case occasionally, not an invitation to actually watch him question a suspect.

"Can George spare you for a while?"

I had the feeling Grandpa would be glad to get rid of me. "Let me check."

As I entered the back room, I followed the sound of voices to find Grandpa and Aput facing off.

Grandpa said, "So, you're the one who put the crazy idea of a new supplier into my granddaughter's head."

Aput was wide-eyed, staring at Grandpa as though afraid the older man might fire him.

I stepped forward. "Aput cares about this place. He only made a suggestion based on some research he's been doing. I mean, imagine that, Grandpa. An employee spending his off-time working on ways to make the place more profitable!" I put a hand on my grandfather's arm to calm him. "Aput is a fantastic and rare employee."

Grandpa opened his mouth to argue but glanced back at Aput and must have registered his stricken expression. He shut his mouth again, skirted around us both, and stomped off.

"Thanks." Aput let out a heavy sigh.

"No thanks necessary. I'm just telling it like it is. It'll be okay. I told Grandpa not to worry about the supplier change. I'm not going to mess with any of his systems or anything again." I glanced around to be sure the old man was gone and leaned closer. "We'll do our best to keep things going smoothly, okay? I know Grandpa's forgetting things a lot lately."

Aput nodded. "Okay. I get it, and you're right. We'll take care of things without upsetting him. There's no need for that."

I smiled, grateful he understood and agreed with my plan. "Thanks. Hey, do you mind if I run out for a bit?"

"Nah, go ahead. I can handle things here."

I thanked him again, grabbed my parka, and hurried back to the front. "Okay," I told Jason. "Let's go."

Phil Albertson lived right in town, much to my surprise. I'd envisioned him living way out by himself somewhere, but his house stood on the edge of Frost Peak next to the library. He invited us into the modest but neat kitchen decorated in avocado-green and eyed me with curiosity.

"This is Frankie Banks," Jason said.

I stuck out my hand, and he shook it. "Phil Albertson. But you probably know that since you're in my house. What do you two need?"

"The first thing I want to know is where you were when Lloyd Dawes was killed." Jason pulled out a notebook and pen.

He tipped his head and gave it some thought. "On a video call with my sister in the lower forty-eight. I remember because she called, and I made the mistake of answering. I got stuck talking about her kids for two hours when I wanted to be down in the bunker organizing some new supplies that came in." His eyes lit up. "Would you like to see it?"

"Your bunker?" You could have knocked me over with a peacock feather. I figured a prepper's bunker was his best-kept secret. Like, they only showed it to immediate family and people they were planning on killing or something.

But Phil's bright expression told me that showing us would be similar to opening presents on Christmas morning for him. His whole demeanor had changed with the idea.

Jason's eyes shot me a question. I shrugged. "Sure." I'd never been inside a bunker before. Seemed like it could be a learning experience.

Phil rubbed his hands together and crossed the room to open a door I hadn't noticed. He led the way down a dark stairway. We followed, me feeling glad to have a cop with a gun along for the trip.

As we descended, it got chillier. By the time we stood on the concrete floor at the bottom of the staircase, it was downright cold. I slipped my parka hood back on and stuffed my hands deep in the pockets.

Phil flipped a light switch, and two rows of fluorescents clicked on overhead. It was a bunker, all right; dim, creepy, and freezing. None of that surprised me, but what did was the sheer amount of stuff packed in.

It was a full basement, probably about fifteen hundred square feet, and lined with floor to ceiling metal shelves like the back room at the general store. Everything was arranged in intuitive groupings—canned food, smoked fish, about four dozen toothbrushes and countless tubes of toothpaste, warm clothes, boots, and blankets, toilet paper ... there was more TP than I'd ever seen in one place. Way more than we had in stock at Spitzer's. My eyes bugged at the variation in softness, size, and number of rolls per package.

Phil grinned and gestured. "I installed a composting toilet, so when the worst happens, I'll be able to live in style."

I had no desire to go check out the composting toilet, so I stayed firmly rooted to the spot and looked around. A queen-sized bed sat in the corner next to an end table with a radio on it. A huge bookshelf stuffed to the gills with paperbacks took up half of one wall. I knew it was more books than Frost Peak's tiny library offered. "Wow," I breathed.

"Yep. I can be happy down here for years without ever going topside." He hooked his thumbs in his belt loops. "If there's radiation up there, I should be good till it dissipates."

I was again surprised Phil had agreed to show us this. But then my gaze fell on the gun cabinet. It was stuffed with all kinds of weapons, and a shelf on top sagged with boxes of ammunition. Looked like Phil was well-prepared to get rid of anyone who might come trying to take over his bunker during the apocalypse. So he didn't have a reason not to show anyone.

I gulped.

Jason recovered quicker than I did. "When was the last time you saw Lloyd?"

"Oh, it had been a couple weeks. He used to be a real problem—showing up at all our group meetings and ruining them with his obnoxious nonsense. Running his mouth, talking over me, and going off on ridiculous tangents." His jaw tightened. "I'm glad he's gone, so I don't have to worry about that ever happening again. Not that he'd been doing it lately. I made sure of that."

"How?" Jason reminded me of a cat watching a bird the way his eyes didn't leave Phil's face. He was obviously a good cop, using body language to inform his opinion as much as the guy's spoken words.

"First, I kicked him out. A couple months ago. Banned him from the meetings. He didn't pay his dues for a few months, and I pounced on that and used it as the reason. He couldn't argue, right? And he didn't. But he did vandalize our meeting hall. Toilet papered it and did some graffiti on the outer walls. We don't own that place, so we had to use our board's insurance money to fix it. The board members were hopping mad, so I said I'd handle it." His chin jutted upward. "Took a couple of the bigger dudes from the group with me and paid a visit to Lloyd at home." A smirk played on his lips. "We convinced him to stay away from the meetings, which he did after that."

My eyes darted to meet Jason's, and I knew he was thinking the same thing I was. His next question verified it. "How'd you convince him? Did you and your guys rough him up?"

Phil pursed his lips. "That would be illegal. We talked to him, is all."

That didn't ring true, but I wasn't about to say anything. I might be impulsive, but inside an underground bunker with a guy who was armed to the teeth wasn't the place to flap my lips and annoy someone.

Jason wasn't cowed at all. "I'm going to need to check your phone—verify that video call with your sister."

The prepper nodded and motioned to the stairs. "Sure. I'll show you right now."

Relieved to be leaving the underground room, I followed Jason up the stairs. This time, I noticed the multiple locks on the door at the top. The door itself was made of thick concrete.

Yeah, Phil didn't have to worry that he'd shown us the bunker. No one was getting through that door if he was downstairs with it locked unless they had some kind of bomb.

I waited in the kitchen while Phil showed Jason his phone logs, then we left. As soon as we were outside, I said, "What do you think? Do you believe his alibi?"

Jason cut his eyes to me, then away. "His phone log did show a call from his sister around the right time, but it didn't have a record of how long it lasted. It's possible he could have finished the discussion with her and then killed Dawes. I'm going to call the sister in the morning and find out if she can verify what Phil said about how long they talked."

My lips pulled downward as I considered that. "I wouldn't think family members are the most reliable alibi-providers. Wouldn't they be the most likely to lie for their relative? I mean, Phil could call her right now and tell her how to corroborate his story."

"Yep." He studied his feet as we trudged along. "I'll have to take his alibi with a grain of salt."

We were both quiet, thinking, until he stopped and turned toward me. "I need to head to the station. Thanks for coming with me."

The way he looked me in the eyes made my heart speed up. I felt a blush rise in my cheeks and was grateful the parka was pulled tight. And if it didn't hide the color, hopefully he'd think I was cold. "Thanks for taking me with you. I'm sorry it wasn't more productive."

He shrugged. "It all helps. You never know when the puzzle pieces will start to fit together. Until then, it's about gathering the pieces."

That made sense. You couldn't finish a puzzle with missing pieces, after all.

"I wanted to tell you again what a nice time I had last night. But I'm going to need a Monopoly rematch. A tournament, perhaps. I can't leave my reputation to wither on the vine like this."

"So you want to totally sink your gamer reputation by letting me defeat you a couple more times. Sure, why not?" I wanted to offer to cook this time, but not having my own place to do it put a real kink in my style. I flashed to an image of trying to enjoy dinner with a man while my grandfather scowled at us from his armchair.

I needed to make up with Grandpa. And think about getting my own place.

"Big talk, but talk is cheap." He winked. "I'll get with you later to figure out a time." With an adorably sweet smile, he headed off.

"Wait!" When he turned back toward me, I said, "You should talk to Carla Swanson. She had motive to kill Lloyd too."

His brows went up a little, but he nodded before leaving.

I watched him go, feeling lighter than I had that morning. I liked Jason. He was handsome and funny, and it seemed like he liked me too. Plus, my friendship with Nina was growing, and it had been nice to see Kaia. Maybe things would work out for me in Frost Peak after all. Even though I kept running up against dead-ends on the Dawes case, Jason was right. We'd find the right puzzle piece soon, and the picture would emerge.

Things were going to be okay.

I smiled and returned to the store with a bouncier step.

Chapter 14

I decided to enter the store through the back door because I wanted to check the snowmobiles. Nina and a friend of hers had gone out to gas up the one I'd left for dead and bring it back, and I wanted to make sure it was there. It was, sitting how it had been when I took it. I made a mental note to check that the radio was on the charger in the office too.

A note flapped on the back door. That was weird. Maybe a delivery had come before we were open or something, and they'd left a note? I pulled it down, my stomach flopping like it contained bad sushi as I read the words: *You shouldn't have come here. You'll regret it.*

I jerked my head up and spun around, scanning the area for anyone who might have left the note. It was dim, as always, but I saw no one, and nothing moved.

Glancing at the note again, I thought about how Jason said someone had left a tip for him that I'd killed Dawes. This must be the same person.

My previous high spirits sank like a stone in a puddle. There it was again—the concern that I'd made the wrong decision moving here. My emotions were like a Yo-Yo, and somebody was doing loop-de-loops with it.

Gravity pulled down on my shoulders. I reread the chicken-scratched words. Was this a threat on my life? Someone who thought I'd killed Lloyd and intended to take some sort of negative action against me in retaliation? Was I in danger?

Then another sobering thought sliced through my mind. If someone planned to hurt me, what if Grandpa or Aput was also around when it happened? *Oh, no.* I could hardly stand the thought they might be in danger because I'd gotten myself into hot water.

Why had I argued with Lloyd that first day I was back? It had been so typically, self-righteously Frankie of me. I'd opened my mouth, made threats without understanding all the aspects of social life in Frost Peak. I'd made myself a prime suspect in the man's murder, and now I might have put my friends and family at risk.

With a heavy sigh, I crinkled the note. The moment I did, an image jolted into my head. It was sharper than any dream I'd had in my life and came with the unsettling feeling that it wasn't from my own subconscious.

It was being presented to me.

Ice everywhere. Cold. And the unmistakable feeling of dread. I didn't know how, but I knew beyond a shadow of a doubt that death was coming.

The flash was gone as fast as it had come, leaving me trembling so hard the crumpled paper fell from my hand. I knelt to retrieve it, thoughts racing. What was that? A vision of some kind? Was it something that had occurred already or a premonition of the future? Or was it a weird daydream, totally random and created by my mind, brought on by the creepy note?

I straightened, swept the area again, and hurried inside. I shut the door and leaned back against it, trying to wrestle my emotions under control but not having much luck.

What in the world had just happened to me? I considered the options again—a premonition, a flashback, a daydream? Could it possibly have anything to do with my magical abilities? I didn't remember ever having such a clear, sudden vision before. It seemed like it could have been brought on by the paper I'd crumpled.

My hand hovered over the pocket I'd stuffed the note into, and I considered pulling it back out, flattening it, and re-crumpling to see if anything weird happened again. But I lowered my hand without retrieving the paper. I didn't *want* it to happen again. At least not until I had my nerves in some kind of control.

Dimly, I recognized the sounds of the store. Of customers milling around. Aput's laughter reached my ears. I straightened. Was there anything I could do to protect them from whoever had left me the threatening note?

What about a protection spell? Was that a thing? It had to be, right? Witches must need to ward off threats sometimes, and why wouldn't they be able to use magic to do it?

I whirled around and went back outside. Still no sign of anyone around. I jogged about fifteen feet away from the building and turned back to face it.

A protection spell. I twisted my lips in thought, wondering how to do a protection spell.

Okay, let's approach this logically. Nina had told me to envision as clearly as possible what I wanted my magic to accomplish, then push some intention into it. I shouldn't think about how it was going to be achieved, only the end result.

I drew a breath of frigid air and considered what I wanted to happen.

Protection. Like, a barrier around the building and people inside against someone aiming to harm them. Thick and impenetrable. A layer of safety around Grandpa and Aput.

When I had the clearest idea I could of the shield I wanted my spell to create, I lifted a hand, did a slightly more flourish-y flourish than I'd done for the sponge spell in the hangar, and released my intention with a whisper. My pulse raced as I waited to see the result.

For a moment, it seemed like nothing would happen. Everything was quiet and still. Then movement near the bottom of the building caught my eye. I peered closer, then moved forward for a better look. Something green, like vines, but no—it wasn't a lovely, natural green color. It was sickly green. Rotten lemon-lime. As though the nineteen-eighties made a baby with the Hulk and produced a completely unnatural, horrible color.

The texture wasn't the same as plants' either. It looked more like... I stepped even closer, and the stuff moved faster, climbing the building's walls at a good clip now. A tortured groan escaped me. The stuff looked like slime. A wall of thick, disgusting, putrid-looking green slime was rapidly enveloping the building. In a few moments, it would make an impenetrable—I assumed, from my visualization, anyway—wall that no one could get through. From the inside or the outside.

Not only would my grandfather and Aput be safe from anyone outside the store looking to harm them, but they'd also be stuck with whoever was already inside. And they'd all be unable to leave. What if the person who'd threatened me was in there with them? Should I run in now, before I got locked out? I didn't know what to do.

Oh, why did I even try this? I had yet to do a spell completely right, and here I was thinking I could do something as complicated as a protection spell on my own. I was a rotten, worthless witch. I should hang up my broom. Or spells or whatever. No one had given me a broom.

Then something occurred to me. I hadn't received a broom, but I *had* gotten a familiar. Maybe Ragnar could help. He'd handled the glacier for me when I botched that spell—a little impenetrable slime should be no problem for him.

What had he said about always being near? Did he mention I could call him if I needed him? I'd never had to before. For the glacier and the wolves, he'd appeared out of nowhere.

I whirled around, searching for a glimpse of him, but nothing stirred. It didn't seem like he'd be arriving soon enough to help me fix this if I couldn't do something to summon him.

But how?

"Ragnar?" I called. But not too loudly because I didn't know who else was around to hear. For all I knew, whoever'd left the note could be watching. I glanced over my shoulder and squeaked when I saw the slime had made it about a quarter of the way up the building. Soon, it would start moving over the windows, and people inside would notice. That was all I needed. Visions of various science fiction movies —the old, cheesy types—danced through my thoughts.

When I turned back forward, Ragnar stood a foot in front of me. "How did you..." I waved it off. "Never mind. That's for later. I messed up a spell." I jerked a thumb over my shoulder. "Any way you could end the slime attack on the store?"

Ragnar chuffed. Being laughed at by a magical polar bear, again, rankled, I'm not going to lie, but I bit back a snarky retort—again. I deserved to be mocked for doing such a ridiculous thing—again.

I was beginning to see a pattern.

The great big polar bear ambled forward, focused on the slime, and made a series of grunts, groans, and growls. The slime's advance halted, hovering in place for a moment before creeping backward and down to the ground once more. Ragnar turned to face me.

"Thanks. I feel like I'm always thanking you." My eyes popped wide. "Hold on!" I rushed past him into the store before he could answer. As I slipped around the counter and down the candy aisle, I glanced around. There were a few shoppers looking at items. Grandpa stood with his back to me, warming his hands by the woodstove. I didn't see Aput. Thankfully, no one acted like they'd noticed a green slime attack on the outer perimeter.

I grabbed a bag of gummy bears and scooted out the back door.

Ragnar was still there, giving me a quizzical look. I tore open the bag and held them out. "I promised you these the next time I saw you. So here you go."

He stuck his nose in the back and slurped up some bears, half-closing his eyes as he sat back to chew on them. *Scrumptious*, he thought to me once he finished chewing.

I lifted the bag enticingly. "More?"

He moved his head back and forth. *I'll take the rest home.*

"Ah. Good call. Draw out the enjoyment."

He shook his head like a fly had landed on his ear, even though it was way too cold for them to be out. Then he pinned me with a direct look. *Why was that horrible stinky goo all over the building?*

Stinky? I didn't notice... Ragnar's expression grew more stern. *Um, spell gone wrong. I was trying to protect my grandpa and Aput. I can't seem to do magic right. Thanks again for helping me undo that. I would have been in some serious doo-doo if you hadn't.*

Doo-doo? Humans have odd speech patterns.

I laughed, but it was forced. Misery crept into my mood, where half an hour ago good feelings about my new life had surged. "You know," I said out loud, "I think it might have been a mistake for me to come here. I can't help but think I'm turning out to be more of a hassle for my grandpa than a help."

Ragnar moved his front paws forward until he was lying down, so his eyes were a few inches below mine. He looked up at me. *You're wrong, my witch.*

I pressed my lips together, holding in the words, even though I wanted to question how on earth he could be so sure. To keep from arguing, I grabbed a couple gummy bears and shoved them in my mouth. Red and green. Yum. Maybe Ragnar was onto something with this being his favorite type of candy. I hadn't had them in a while, and I'd been missing out.

You do belong here. It's your destiny to be here. To meet me and help George.

How can you be so sure?

One of the mysteries of magic and the spirits of the North.

I aimed an annoyed look at him. *So mysterious. You know, if magic wasn't so baffling, maybe spells would be easier for me, and I'd stop almost ruining the general store.*

Ragnar rose to his giant feet, much more gracefully than you'd think such a huge animal could. *You are only a baby witch. Ruining a building or two is to be expected.* He ambled away at a leisurely pace. *It's good you called me.*

Wait! You came so fast. Can you teleport or something?

He chuffed out his funny laugh. *No. I try to stay fairly close to you. I can move faster than a normal polar bear, and I can hear you however softly you call. But I can't teleport.* He started away again.

Wait!

He paused and gave me a curious look.

Is having visions part of my magic? I think I might have had one. About ice and... Well, it wasn't very nice. But I don't know if it was my imagination or something real.

His nose wrinkled, and then he sniffed the air. Suddenly, he galloped to me, skidding to a halt at the last possible second. He snatched the bag of gummies from my hand, though I tried to get it back to grab a couple more candies. *I'm afraid I don't know the answer to that.* He loped away, carrying the gummy bears between his teeth.

I rubbed my arms and watched him go, glad the slime was gone but wishing for more help with the magic. When I turned to go back inside, Timber sat between me and the door. His black nose twitched.

"Oh. Hi. Did you, um, see all that?"

He tipped his head, adorably, like a dog when you ask if they want a treat. But he didn't answer.

I blew out a breath. "If you did, I don't suppose I could convince you not to tell my grandfather?"

He tipped his head the opposite way.

"I didn't think so." I stopped to rub his ears as I passed, and he leaned in. Maybe he'd keep my secrets. Maybe not. Either way, I had bigger things to worry about.

Chapter 15

For the rest of the day, I put my head down and worked. I watched for a moment to talk to Grandpa, but for an older guy, he was pretty spry when it came to dodging around displays and into aisles whenever I got close. It was obvious he was avoiding me.

Fine. I'd let him get away with it for now. But at some point, I was going to use the skills I'd gained playing ninja superhero with my friends in the neighborhood I grew up in and corner him. He was going to accept my apology and sincere promise not to mess with his inventory systems again, or I was going to make a fool of myself blubbering about it until he did.

That was my plan, and I was determined to see it through. Grandpa being upset with me hurt too much to do anything different.

Plus, I'd been thinking about it while I tried to make bare shelves look fuller and hunted for nonexistent replenishments for out-of-stock items in the back. Something had to be done about this issue. Mickey Grimes' new store in Cross Creek was going to bankrupt us easily if we didn't make rapid changes to the inventory and supply.

I had to figure out a way to get it done without upsetting Grandpa. That part was non-negotiable. Like I'd told Aput, Grandpa was elderly, and I didn't want him distressed. We were simply going to have to figure out how to get things done around him.

At the end of the day, I trudged upstairs, tired and defeated. I showered with water as hot as I could stand, and then stood under it until it began to cool. Then I braided my hair, pulled on my baby blue flannel pajamas with panda bears all over them—that made me feel guilty, and I vowed to order polar bears next time—and considered sitting under my happy light for a while. Maybe that would make me feel better. But I didn't want to be awake all night, so I curled up on the sofa with my feet under me. After staring at the wall for ten minutes, I huffed out an irritated breath and grabbed the TV remote.

"Find a good movie, will ya, girl?"

I twisted to see my grandfather approaching from the kitchen, a heaping bowl of popcorn in his hands. "Sure." I scooted over, and he sat next to me with the bowl on the cushion between us.

He inclined his head toward the snack. "Help yourself."

"Thanks." I munched while scanning the channel guide. I found a murder mystery that was just starting and switched the channel. "Wow, this popcorn is good."

"I sprinkled some of that canned cheese stuff on it," he rumbled. "Has too much sodium and a bunch of ingredients I can't pronounce, but it's tasty."

"I love ingredients you can't pronounce." I stuffed a handful of popcorn into my mouth and kept the hand under my chin to catch crumbs.

"Your grandmother always wanted to read labels and only eat what she knew and understood. Rest her soul. She was the best woman in the world, save for your mother, but it was hard for her living up here. We don't have a lot of whole, fresh foods to choose from in the winter, you know."

I nodded, keeping my lips zipped over the words that wanted to come out, which were, "Better suppliers might be able to help with that." There, see? I'd managed to keep that gem to myself. I could totally follow my plan to avoid upsetting him. Easy peasy.

"What aren't you saying?"

I started and shot him a look. The skin around his eyes crinkled, like he was holding back a smile. "Nothing. Why do you ask?" I stuffed more popcorn into my mouth, hoping he'd drop it.

"I can tell when you aren't telling me everything. It's about inventory, isn't it?"

I made a noncommittal gesture and pointed at my mouth to let him know I couldn't answer without being rude and spewing crumbs all over.

Grandpa chuckled. "You're a firecracker like your mother. Like your grandmother too. You'd think I'd have learned I can't win against any of you by now."

I leaned my head on the back of the couch. "I don't want to win against you, Grandpa. It's not a competition."

He smiled and watched the TV for a minute. Then he said, "I met with my lawyer today. Should have done it a while ago, but, you know, people do tend to avoid this type of thing."

"What lawyer? What type of thing?"

He didn't make eye contact with me. "I fixed my will. Made sure you were the beneficiary on my life insurance too." He patted my hand in the popcorn dish. "You'll be all set if something happens to me, honey."

Immediately, my eyes misted. I shook my head and opened my mouth to object, but he squeezed my hand. "Don't worry. I'm not planning on kicking the bucket this week or anything. But I'm getting older, and I want you taken care of. So I handled it today, that's all. I just wanted you to know." He winked. "You get the store too, so if you decide to keep it, you can do whatever you want about inventory then."

I pursed my lips and didn't say anything. He grabbed the remote and turned up the volume. We ate and watched in silence, but I wasn't following the movie. All I could think about was my grandfather not being around anymore. And how maybe my being there could accelerate that event; someone had left that threatening note. I could be in danger and bring that danger to his doorstep too.

During a commercial, I turned toward him. "Grandpa, when I came back to the store this morning, I found a note on the back door." I pulled the crumpled paper from my pocket, where I'd transferred it earlier, and showed him.

He peered at the messy writing through his reading glasses. "Huh," he said mildly, handing it back and getting more popcorn from the bottom of the bowl.

"Huh? That's all you have to say about it?"

He glanced at me and shrugged. "What should I say?"

"I think this is aimed at me. Someone thinks I killed Lloyd, and they're threatening me. I'm worried about you and Aput, that's all." My heart squeezed again at the thought they might be in danger.

Grandpa still didn't look concerned. "It could have been meant for me or Aput too. It's someone feeling sassy, putting up a note to scare us. Could even be that Mickey Grimes, trying to goad us into closing down outright, so he can have all the business for his new place. I wouldn't worry about it, honey. Besides, don't forget I have magic too." He smirked. "I can handle myself pretty decently most days." He pointed at the screen. "Shh. Show's back on."

But it turned out a murder mystery was the last thing I wanted to watch. I excused myself and headed to my bedroom, prepared to toss and turn all night, worrying. But then something Grandpa had said returned to my mind, and I latched onto it. It gave me an idea.

Life insurance. Had Lloyd Dawes had any? If he did, could the beneficiary have killed him?

I glanced at the clock and winced. After eleven. Too late to call or text Jason and ask him about it. I left my room again, heading for the kitchen. Maybe a dose of chamomile tea would help me sleep.

As I waited for the water to boil, I leaned on the doorframe and watched the end of the show. The gardener did it with a hoe. *Classic.* I'd figured that out before the second commercial, and I was only half listening.

If only real murders were as easy to solve.

The next morning, I woke early and counted down the minutes until it was a socially appropriate time to text Jason about whether Lloyd had a life insurance policy.

I kept my phone nearby while I ate and got ready for the day, but Jason didn't text back. By the time I was ready to leave the flat, my patience was gone. I wasn't supposed to work until around eleven. Maybe I should walk over to the police department and try to find Jason.

Halfway to the station, I decided to try a different tactic. I'd seen Molly Dawes cleaning in Mickey's office building that time. Maybe she was there this morning, and I could talk to her directly.

Molly hadn't been very nice to me at the Founder's Day celebration, and I was apprehensive about seeking her out. But she was Lloyd's sister, so it stood to reason she'd know the most about him. Without giving it too much thought, I changed directions and headed for the office building.

When I got there, I scooted out of the lobby fast, not wanting to deal with Mickey or having to talk to a receptionist who might page Molly or something. I darted into the first hallway I saw and made my way down, looking for the cleaning cart.

It took twenty minutes and a lot of trekking up and down hallways plus finding a different cleaning person first, but I eventually came upon Molly Dawes' cart in a hallway at the back of the building. She was inside a small conference room, scrubbing coffee rings off a long table. She looked up when I entered, then wiped sweat from her brow and straightened. "What are you doing here? There's nothing scheduled for this room today." Her tone was hard, her jaw set firm.

"Actually, I was looking for you." At her suspicious expression, I hurried to add, "I saw you cleaning in this building the other day, so I thought I might be able to find you here." I stepped into the room. "I was hoping to talk to you about your brother." She opened her mouth, but I held up a hand. "I know you think I had something to do with his death, and I can understand why you think that. I did have a public argument with him soon before he was killed. But I didn't kill him; in fact, I have a strong interest in figuring out who did. I don't want my grandfather's store's reputation to suffer. Plus, I want the killer caught, of course."

She eyed me while slowly swooping the cleaning cloth in a circle, basically moving cleaner around without the elbow grease to back it up. "If you were the murderer, you'd want to pin it on someone else. How do I know that isn't what you're working on doing?"

"You don't, I guess." I shrugged. "All I can say is I'm here to help my grandfather with his business." *And get over being left at the altar.* I pushed that thought away. "That's it. And maybe make a friend or two along the way. I was angry with your brother, that much is true. I didn't want him stealing from my grandpa. But that doesn't mean I'd kill him. I barely kill spiders."

"My brother was way more annoying than a spider." She refocused on her work, scrubbing harder.

Did that mean she'd agreed to talk to me? I ventured a question. "Did Lloyd have life insurance?"

"Ha! I highly doubt it. You have to care about someone to buy life insurance and name a beneficiary. Lloyd didn't care about anyone but himself. He wouldn't spend a dime trying to make sure another person was okay after he died." She worked even harder on the coffee ring, and I began to fear for the table's finish.

The way she talked about her brother jolted me. It wasn't the most loving tone, but then again, it fit with what everyone else in town seemed to think of the man.

Molly glanced up and must have read my thoughts in my expression because she said, "He may have been my flesh and blood, but Lloyd was a jerk. Ever since we were kids."

"Do you have other family?"

Her jaw clenched and unclenched. "Not anymore. Just me and him left. Only me now, I guess." She picked up the spray bottle and stalked past me to the cart. "I'm off duty now."

That made sense. Most office cleaners worked overnight. I followed Molly as she pushed her cart to the elevator, then I got on with her. As we descended, I started thinking about the jacket I'd seen downstairs when I visited Mickey. "Do you know where Mr. Grimes is today?"

She shook her head. The elevator stopped, dinged, and the door slid open. She pushed the cart forward. "He said he needed to leave town for a while. Told me to keep up my cleaning schedule, and he'd have his receptionist cut my check."

I followed her to a supply room, where she stowed the cart, thinking it was a little suspicious that the developer had decided to leave town now. Was he trying to escape everyone's notice during the investigation? *Drat!* I wished I could have seen that jacket closer the first time I was there.

Molly pulled on a parka and headed outside, and I followed along, not having much else to do. She walked toward a pick-up truck in the lot, and I noticed it had a bunch of gear in the back. "Are you going somewhere?"

"Ice fishing."

That's right. I'd heard she was a good fisherwoman. "That sounds fun." It didn't. "When are you going?"

Hand on the door handle, she turned to regard me. "Five in the morning. You can come if you want. It'd be a good way to see what kind of gear you need to keep in supply at the store. Lots of subsistence fishers up here."

I considered it for a moment but shook my head. "That's a little too bright and early for me. Not bright, though—it's never bright at this time of year. But thanks for the invitation."

"Suit yourself. If you change your mind, I'll be going to Stony Lake. Leaving Ace Top apartment building around four forty-five."

With a nod and a wave, I saw her off, then turned to walk home, still thinking about that button and where Mickey Grimes had gone. How could I find out?

My phone buzzed, and I fumbled around to get it out of my pocket, get my mitten off, and answer. It was Jason. "Sorry I didn't text back right away. I was playing pick-up basketball at the gym and didn't see it until now. What's up?"

"I had a thought and wanted to run it by you. Did Lloyd have a life insurance policy?"

"Not that I've come across."

So Molly was telling the truth. "I really think we need to focus in on Mickey Grimes." I didn't want to tell him about the jacket with the missing button—I wasn't sure about it, and it made me sound like a stalker. Or, at least, like I'd been doing solo investigating I shouldn't have been. But it nudged Mickey the highest on my list over Carla and Phil.

"I'm working on it," he answered. "I'll let you know if I find anything substantial."

"Thanks." We hung up as I arrived back at the store just in time for my shift. Sleuthing would have to be put on hold while I straightened goods and checked people out.

But the whole time, I knew I'd be thinking about Mickey and that missing button.

Chapter 16

M y eyes popped open, and it was still pitch black in my room.
Not that it ever got very much brighter at this time of year, but
it was immediately clear to me that it was early. With a groan, I twisted
my hips around to look at the clock. Four am. Ugh. I rolled back over
and closed my eyes, breathing slow and deep in an attempt to go back
to sleep.

Four o'clock. Fishing's at five.

My eyes sprang open again. Fishing? I racked my brain, trying to
figure out where the thought had come from. Still feeling sluggish, I
rolled over again. My back gave a twinge, and I sighed before
scooching this way and that to adjust myself into a better position.

Five o'clock. You could fish and get back in time for breakfast.

Oh, right. Molly's ice fishing expedition was in just under an hour.
When I'd gone to bed, I'd had no intention of getting up for it. In
fact, I hadn't even thought about it after declining the invitation the
previous morning.

So why was my subconscious pricking me about it now?

I tried to push it away but remembered what she'd said—maybe I
could get a better feel for what folks in Frost Peak needed for their ice
fishing excursions. It made sense, from a customer service perspective.
And to fight the ding my reputation had taken. Being out and about
in the community, doing what people here did was good PR.

I shoved into a seated position and evaluated myself. Yep, I was wide awake. There was no going back to sleep now, so I might as well go. I flipped on the light and found my phone on the end table to figure out where Molly's apartment building was. It would take me about ten minutes to walk there, so I had time for a quick bite to eat and to pack some water and a snack.

When I was ready to go, I grabbed a pen to leave Grandpa a note. *Where's all the scrap paper?* I pawed through the junk drawer, looked on the table, and checked the end tables by the sofa but couldn't find anything suitable to write on. There was some paper in my room, but a glance at the wall clock told me I was cutting the timing on this pretty close.

Reasoning that I wasn't scheduled to work until eleven and would have my phone on me, I hurried toward the door.

But an image of Grandpa, feeling worried about where I'd disappeared to, sprang to mind, and I groaned and raced to my bedroom for scrap paper. After I'd scrawled down *Stony Lake with Molly Dawes*, I raced out of the flat.

Ten minutes later, I waved at Molly as she headed toward her truck, a backpack slung over her shoulder. She stopped and waited for me, surprise evident on the small bit of her face I could see inside the parka hood and behind the big round glasses. "You came."

"Yeah, you were right about me seeing more of what it's like here. I'm excited to try. But go easy on me—I'm a total newbie."

She hoisted the backpack over the side rail into the bed of the truck. "People learn fast here, or they get hurt." At my shocked expression, her face broke into a wide smile. "I'm kidding. It isn't dangerous. The ice is nice and thick, and I have a little shanty out there." She gestured toward a cooler in the back. "I have beer and snacks. It's like being at the spa. With fish."

Before I could figure out anything even semi-appropriate to say back to that, Molly jumped into the truck, and I hurried to clamber up into the passenger seat.

We were off.

Awkward silence filled the cab. I thought about how Molly worked for Mickey and tried to work out how I could get more information about him. Remembering how he'd come over during the Founder's celebration and said that Molly had told him she thought I'd killed Lloyd, I wondered if he'd been the one to leave the note on the back door of the shop.

He must have been. The button I'd found near where Lloyd was killed had matched the jacket in Mickey's office.

I gave Molly a sidelong glance, took a deep breath, and decided to give it a try. "How long have you worked for Mr. Grimes?"

"Few years."

"He must be a decent boss, then."

She shrugged with one shoulder and didn't answer that.

"Do you know much about him?"

"He signs my checks."

Tough nut.

I chewed my lip and watched the scenery go by out the window, trying to figure out what to ask next. The silence got so oppressive I couldn't take it anymore and burst out, "I'm so sorry, again, about your brother. I can't imagine how you must feel. I mean, I don't have siblings, so I really can't imagine. But I can imagine, though, because I'm a human person. I mean, I have empathy and all that." I stammered to a halt, face burning. I was prattling. Molly seemed to be ignoring me, focusing on the road. "I'm sorry," I ended lamely.

She cut her eyes to me for a second. "Yeah. Like I said, Lloyd was a jerk. It's a wonder he lived as long as he did, I suppose. Always irritating people. Obnoxious. He was also completely inept. That's why he couldn't hold down a job or be a productive member of society in any way. All he could do was go down his doomsday rabbit hole and try to drag others with him. Half of it was real madness, and the other half was a racket. Trying to get money out of people that he didn't have to earn."

Okay, that had been a lot of words. Maybe we were getting somewhere.

"I heard Mickey Grimes wanted Lloyd out of that house." I used a gentle tone, mindful that as much as she'd said she hadn't cared for Lloyd, the man was her brother. She'd certainly been upset at the hall when she'd accused me of killing him, so there must be some feelings there. "Do you know anything about that? About Lloyd fighting with Mickey, I mean."

She turned the wheel to the left to get around a tight corner, faster than I appreciated, and I held onto the door to keep from flopping over.

"Yeah, Mickey wanted that house back. He offered Lloyd a good deal on an apartment in the building I'm in, but my dense brother wouldn't take it. He didn't want to live in a cracker box, he'd said. Needed to be out on some property for when the worst happened. I guess a house is safer from aliens than an apartment." She rolled her eyes.

"Yeah." I had no idea what type of dwelling was safer from aliens. "I can see not wanting to leave your home, I guess. Bet that made Mickey mad, though."

"He wasn't happy, that's for sure."

"Molly, do you think Mickey might have killed your brother? To finally get him off the property?"

Her eyelids fluttered in surprise. "Never thought of that."

Was that an answer? This woman was tougher to talk to than a mime in Central Park.

Then she continued, "You know, Mickey was nice to me after Lloyd died. Had me in his office to sit and talk about it." She slid her eyes my way briefly. "That's when I told him I thought you'd killed him. Sorry about that. But he was a good listener. Acted like he cared."

"That's nice." Did he care? Or was he looking for a scapegoat?

She pulled off the street into a parking lot with snow piled high in a ring around all the edges. A frozen lake waited for us, dotted with several ice shanties. Some looked like tents and others appeared wooden.

Molly threw the truck in park, twisted the key to shut off the truck, and hopped out.

Guess I'm supposed to follow her. I got out, slower, and rounded the end of the truck. Molly had jumped into the bed and was scooting stuff to the end. "Grab those buckets, will you?"

I complied, pulling off the two buckets outfitted with cushions attached to the closed ends. I guessed they would be our seats.

Molly got down, grabbed a heater, fishing poles, a tackle box, and a small duffle bag and headed for the ice. I had to hurry to catch up with her, and I was carrying far less than she was.

There was a moment of panic when I stepped onto the ice, and I wished my hands were free both to balance with and to catch me if I went tumbling heels over tea kettle. Or however that saying went.

By contrast, Molly didn't even slow as she made the transition, obviously well used to handling herself on the frozen lake. She took normal strides, which were pretty long because she was tall. I stuck to tiny little shuffling steps, my body tense. Ten or twenty yards out onto the ice, I felt like I had the hang of it, and I was able to catch up with Molly, who had already ducked into an ice shanty. Hers was a small blue tent shaped like an upside-down cone, as though a giant had dropped their ice cream onto the frozen lake.

I stuck my head through the gap in the tent and found Molly arranging her tackle box and other gear. She glanced at me. "Set those down by the hole, will you?"

I didn't love the authoritative tone, but I nodded and entered the shanty. I dropped one bucket on its side, mumbled an apology, and fumbled around trying to get both seats set upright. My thick mittens didn't make the job easier. When I was done, I stood awkwardly for a moment, feeling like there was something else I should do to help get ready for the ice fishing. But since I didn't have the first clue what that would be, and Molly hadn't asked me to do anything additional, I simply sank onto my bucket and observed her.

Watching Molly prepare to ice fish was like watching an Olympic diver plan and execute a gold-metal maneuver. All her movements were fluid and sure, as though she'd done them around a million times, and I figured she had. She was on autopilot.

When the silence became too much, I said, "Where did you live before you moved to Frost Peak?"

"Canada, the interior," she answered.

I was beginning to understand that Molly tended to use the fewest number of words possible to answer questions. It was as though she was the opposite of her brother in that respect. Of course, I'd only seen him in action once, but I didn't think his mouth had stopped moving the whole time.

"Why did you move here?"

She kept her eyes on what she was doing with the fishing pole— messing with the line or something—and shrugged a shoulder. "I got tired of that one-horse town." She barked out a laugh. "So I moved to a second one-horse town. I'm not built for cities."

"It must've been nice for you and your brother to travel together," I suggested.

She shook her head sharply. "We didn't come together—Lloyd followed me here."

"That's kind of nice. He must've really liked being around you."

That drew a snort. She set the fishing pole through a hook I hadn't seen before on the side of her bucket and rested her forearms on her knees. "After our mother died, I didn't want to be around there anymore. I didn't want to be around him either, but he'd appeared about a week after I'd arrived here. I guess, without Mother or me around, Lloyd must have gotten spooked. He always did need somebody nearby to take care of him. Guy was an idiot when it came to most things. No common sense at all." Her mouth twisted in derision.

I had no idea what to say. Even though Molly wasn't speaking too highly of him, I didn't want to disparage the dead, especially right in front of his sister, by agreeing with her assessment. Sometimes, people said all kinds of bad things about their family members but didn't appreciate it at all when someone else did the same.

So I was glad when Molly scooted forward on her bucket, tipped her head, and peered into the hole. "More ice has formed in there than I thought," she said with a small frown. "Better enlarge the hole." She got up and dug around in the duffle bag for several moments, finally drawing out a tool. As she returned to the hole and started to bang on the ice around its edges, I shivered. Something about that tool was triggering my creepiness factor. It was red-painted metal, a couple feet long, with a round, metal hammer-head on the end.

It made short work of enlarging the hole, and soon, Molly sat back, looking satisfied. "That's better." She set the tool on the ice next to her bucket and eyed me. "How about you? You moved here to help your grandfather, right?"

I nodded, dragging my eyes away from the ice-pounding tool. "My grandmother died a few months back, and Grandpa has been having issues with his memory. He and I both thought it would be good for him to have a helper here. Plus, I had some ... things not going right in California anyway, so I figured it was time for a change." I didn't want to discuss Chad with Molly. It seemed way too personal.

She bobbed her head up and down. "I can relate to that." She kept her eyes on the hole, watching the fishing pole for signs of movement. "You know, I've been thinking lately it would be nice for me to have more friends." She flicked her eyes up to meet mine. "Thanks for coming today. It's kind of nice to have some company for once."

"Thanks for inviting me. I think you were right about it being a good thing for me to see what people do here firsthand. It's important to me that we keep the shop stocked with exactly what folks want and need. Especially since Mr. Grimes is going to be opening a new store in Cross Creek."

She leaned back on the bucket. "I heard about that. Mr. Grimes sure is excited about it—it's all he's been talking about lately. I think he's going to want me to consider going to work there, but I'm not sure I want to move. And I know I don't want to travel to Cross Creek and back every day during the winter."

"I don't blame you." And not just because I really didn't want anyone to agree to work at Mr. Grimes' new place. "Have you worked for him the entire time you've lived in Frost Peak?"

"Pretty much. I did a few odd cleaning jobs on my own when I first got here, but he tracked me down pretty fast and asked me to work for him. He doesn't pay all that well, but it's steady work, and he's always developing new businesses, so I figure the work will never dry up, you know?"

That made sense. Living up here, it wasn't like there was a corporation on every corner for people to land good-paying, long-term positions. "Smart. And good for you." I didn't add that I thought working for Mickey Grimes was probably the last thing I'd do if I moved to Frost Peak without a job. Because, of course, that wasn't true. I only didn't want to work for him now because he had been a jerk to me, was threatening my grandfather's business, and had probably killed a man and framed me for it. Molly hadn't had all those experiences with the man when she'd moved here, so it was natural for her to accept a position with him. "Is he a pretty good guy to work for?"

She shrugged. "He's a boss. Not a particularly great one, but not awful either. He pretty much leaves me alone to do my thing as long as I don't spend too much money on cleaning supplies. And he's interested in my life—asks me questions about how I'm doing and stuff. Like I was telling you how he talked to me about Lloyd. That's more than most people around here do." That deep frown appeared on her face again, touching what I could see of her forehead and wrinkling it. "Mostly, I'm invisible to everyone."

I felt a stab of empathy for Molly. Moving to a small town with only one or two people who really knew you wasn't easy to do. I was originally from Frost Peak and still had family here, and it had been tough for me. In fact, within twenty-four hours of being here, I was a murder suspect.

Molly reached over and opened the cooler. She pulled out of a can of beer and held it out to me.

My eyes popped wide. It was like, six in the morning. I shook my head. "I better not. I have to work later today."

"Suit yourself." She shrugged, popping open the can and taking a big swig.

I tried not to look as shocked as I felt. After all, Molly probably wasn't the only one around here who drank beer all day while they were ice fishing. I had a feeling both were pretty common pastimes.

A shiver ran through me, and I huddled tighter on the bucket. Molly noticed and raised an eyebrow. "You cold?"

I nodded. "A little bit. This parka is great, but maybe because I'm not moving around much, I'm getting a little chill."

Molly rose to her feet, more gracefully than you would expect from someone her size. "I have a good jacket in the truck. It's big enough to fit over the one you have on. I'll run and get it for you. Just watch the line, will you? If it starts to bob, pick up the pole, and reel in the fish."

"Oh, but—" But Molly was already gone, heading across the ice toward the parking lot.

I chewed my bottom lip and eyed the fishing pole. I'd never been fishing, ice or otherwise, and I didn't relish the thought of having to fight with one here in this ice shanty. I sent up a silent plea that the fish would stay away until Molly got back.

Was the pole bobbing? It had moved a tiny bit—I could tell because a tag attached to it had fluttered.

I glanced out the flap Molly had left open to see if she was returning, and suddenly, a strange feeling overtook me. As I looked at the expanse of ice, I was thrown back into the vision I'd had outside the general store. Dread filled me like it had during those flashes. What was going on?

My mind started whirling, and I wondered if maybe Mickey was on his way here or something. Was that what was setting off my spidey senses?

I craned to see through the shanty door, hoping not to see another vehicle pulling in. There were no new cars in the lot, but Molly was on her way back toward me, and a long brown jacket hung over one arm.

A brown jacket.

The brown jacket I'd seen hanging in the reception area of Mickey's office building. The one with the missing button.

Chapter 17

My heart rate picked up to a strong gallop, and I glanced down at the tool Molly had used to enlarge the hole in the ice. I looked closer at the hammer end, and an image of Lloyd's body flashed before me. The dent in his skull was the same size and shape as the round part at the end of that rod.

The fishing pole fluttered again, drawing my eye. The paper attached to it had writing on it. I peered at the words Won Pike Tournament scrawled on it. Molly must have wanted to remember which pole helped her win. But the words barely registered. What did was the handwriting. The same as on the note left on the store's back door.

Molly was almost to the ice shanty now, and I surged to my feet. But there was no way past her, and I'd ridden in her truck. What was I going to do?

Molly's gaze met mine, and I tried to rearrange my expression to pleasant companion status, but it was too late. Recognition flowed over her face. An instant after that, her features fell in sadness.

She continued the final few yards as my eyes darted around wildly. How was I going to get out of this? There was no one around, and nothing but ice in three directions. The parking lot was in the fourth direction, but there was nothing there except Molly's truck, and I didn't have the keys. If I ran in that direction, I'd be in the woods soon unless I stayed on the snowy road. I'd get lost in the forest or caught quickly by Molly and her truck on the road.

"I see you figured it out," Molly said as she closed the last bit of distance between us. She ducked past me and hefted the ice tool into her hand. If my heart hadn't already been hammering along near its maximum rate, that would've made it speed up for sure. "It's too bad. I thought I might finally make a friend."

I had to do something. But what that would be, I had absolutely zero idea. So I decided to stick with what I knew best until something better came up. I was nothing if not nosy. "Why did you kill your brother?" I edged my way out of the shanty, not knowing what I'd do outside but definitely not wanting to be stuck in there with her.

Molly cocked her head and hefted the ice tool from one hand to the other. Then she stopped and tossed the brown jacket onto my stool. She followed me out of the tent, and I was afraid she'd forgo answering and simply attack. Instead, she said, "Lloyd is the reason I'm an orphan today. The reason our mother is dead."

"What do you mean?" Partly, I was trying to distract her until I could figure out what to do, but I also really wanted to know what had happened between the siblings.

Great, Frankie. You're in danger of being killed by a madwoman, and you want the gossip. I tried to keep my mind on getting away, inching farther away from the shanty.

"It was back in Canada. Mother needed a new heat exchanger installed on her mobile home. Lloyd was living with her and would've had to pay for part of it, and he didn't want to, so he convinced her he could change it out himself." Her face twisted in rage and something else—grief. "Of course, the idiot installed it backward. Mother's house filled up with carbon monoxide, and she died. I wish he would have been in that house when it happened," she spat. "But, of course, he was out drinking and spreading his ridiculous apocalypse nonsense. When I left, it was more to get away from him than anything, and I couldn't believe it when he'd followed me here. I did everything I could to stay away from him, but he was always bugging me. That day, I was going to the general store to pick up some supplies, including this." She raised the ice-smashing tool. "I went out the back door of the store because it was closer to where I'd left my snowmobile, and Lloyd was back there, leaning on the wall and drinking from a flask. I tried to ignore him and just take off, but he blocked my way. Said he wanted to go back into the store and get some stuff he'd forgotten. He showed me everything in his pockets and cackled about how he'd lifted it—wanted me to go in and help him steal some more stuff. We had an argument, and he was just so ... Lloyd." She said his name like it tasted like her most hated food. "Anyway, I told him no way was I going to help him do something like that. I like Frost Peak, and I like George Spitzer. All I wanted to do was live a quiet life here. Do my cleaning, do my fishing, maybe enter a competition or two, and just live and grow old quietly. I told him I wished he would have stayed in Canada or better yet, that he'd never been born. I shoved him out of my way and started down the path, but he just had to get the last word. He had to mock me. He said it was me who shouldn't have been born. That Mother always liked him best." Her fists clenched around the ice tool, and I could see the rage that she felt when Lloyd had said that to her return to her body. "I didn't even think," she said, speaking softer now. "I turned around, raised my new ice tool, and smashed him on the head with it. It wasn't that I intended to kill him, but I guess I hit him in just the right spot with the right amount of force." Her eyes unfocused for a moment, as though she were living the scene again, and I was shocked when a smile played on her lips. "You should've seen the look on his face right before he crumpled over. He was shocked, but he knew I'd gotten the last word on the matter."

A horrible chill skittered up and down my spine at the coldness in Molly's words. As I watched her eyes refocus and land on me, her mouth hardened into a grim line, and I knew I had to do something, or she would hit me with the very same murder weapon she had used on her brother. I had to get that tool away, but how? Even though she'd just said more words than I'd believed she could utter at once, it was clear Molly was done talking. She took a step toward me.

I backed away, not bothering to move slowly now that her attention was focused on me. *Okay, Frankie. You're a witch. You can manipulate magic, and you are capable of getting that ice tool away from this madwoman.* The self-directed pep-talk helped, and I shoved away niggling thoughts about how I'd never gotten magic to work properly before. Instead, I focused with all my might on the ice tool in Molly's hands. I envisioned it skittering away over the ice, too far in the distance for her to retrieve it.

I continued focusing, even as she advanced and raised the tool, higher and higher. I swallowed hard and forced myself to focus on the image of it flying over the frozen lake. I brought that picture as clearly into my mind as I could. Then, just as she reached the top of the arc and began to bring the tool down toward my head, I lifted my hand and murmured, "Tool of death, go where you're sent," did a simple flourish, and pushed out my intention. Then I held my breath.

Molly's eyes popped open wide as the tool flew from her hands, as though an invisible giant had simply plucked it out of her meaty grasp. The tool flew in a high arc over the icy lake, but it didn't fly away farther than we could see. Instead, it crashed right into Molly's ice shanty. The tent collapsed, torn right down the middle by the weight.

Molly stood comically, hands above her head. She twisted her neck to look upward, as though expecting the tool to still be there. When it wasn't, she dropped both her eyes and hands. She looked at the shanty for an instant before pinning me with the most furious look I'd ever seen on anyone who wasn't acting in a movie. Then, she launched herself at me.

What should I do?

I took too much time thinking about it, and Molly was on me. She knocked me backward, and I hit the ice painfully, right on my tailbone. Luckily, my parka and snow-pants provided some cushion. I didn't think it was broken. Not that I had time to think or even spare a moment of concern for my vertebrae because Molly's snarling face was two inches from mine.

"What happened to being friends?" I gasped.

"You're too nosy to be friends." She tried to get ahold of my wrists, but I twisted and writhed like a snake on hot asphalt, trying to dislodge her from her seat on my legs.

Then I heard it. Far in the distance but completely recognizable.

A roar.

Molly heard it too, and she paused her assault on me for the barest of moments to scan the frozen lake.

I used all my strength to twist my hips and shoulders and was rewarded when Molly toppled off me. I scrambled awkwardly, slipping on the ice in some bazaar crablike maneuver, but somehow, miraculously, I gained my feet. I took off, and with sheer will, ignored it every time a foot shot out in the wrong direction. Somehow, I managed to keep going without falling, and I tried to think of a spell to try next.

From deep inside my parka came a buzz. *My phone!* It had signal. I couldn't believe it. I kept moving but wrestled the phone out of my pocket, pulled off a mitten, and slid the bar to answer Jason's call. Then I slipped the phone back into my pocket and twisted to see where Molly was.

She wasn't far behind me, and the movement I'd made shot me off-balance. Both feet slid out from under me, and I hit the ice, this time banging my elbow.

Molly was on me while I was still sliding. Man, she was much lighter on her feet than I'd expect for someone so heavy—all her weight was on my middle section. She drew back a hand, and I only had a second to jerk my shoulders and neck to the side as her fist barreled toward my face. I managed to move enough that she punched the ice instead and howled in pain.

Another roar cut through the sounds of Molly and me panting, and she froze. The sound was much closer this time. If I could hold out a few more minutes...

I twisted again, shoving hard with my arms at the same time, but this time, Molly was ready and didn't budge. My chest and abdomen screamed at me to get the weight off.

Feeling too weak to wrestle anymore, I did the only thing I could do —imagined Molly flying backward through the air, off of me. I didn't have a lot of time to make sure the visualization was perfect and there was no way I could think of a rhyme, but there wasn't another choice. I had to try. "Why are you doing this?" I groaned.

She looked back at me, as though she'd forgotten I was there when the bear roared. Tipping her head, she said, "Because you know I killed my brother. I can't just let you go."

With my last burst of energy, I wrenched my arm out from under her and gave a weak wrist flourish.

Molly flew off me as though someone had hit her in the abdomen with a battering ram. I watched her fly in a perfect arc and then slam into the ice and slide ten feet.

I did it! I should be running. But I was in awe that I'd made a spell do exactly what I'd wanted it to. I painfully climbed to my feet, grinning like a mad person.

Molly looked at me, and her eyes were wide with fear.

That's right! Fear the big, bad witch. Don't mess with me, or I'll do another spell just right and send you across the lake.

Oh, wait. She wasn't looking at me. She was looking past me. I spun around and found Ragnar, on his hind legs.

I deflated. "Oh. It's you." Molly wasn't afraid of my prowess. She was terrified of Ragnar.

Oh. It's you too. The one I just ran fifteen miles at a dead gallop to save. You're welcome. He dropped to his feet and inclined his nose in Molly's direction. *She's running away.*

I whirled to find out he was right. Molly ran across the ice toward the broken shanty. No, she angled away, toward the parking lot. Where Jason's black SUV sat next to her truck. His door opened.

Ragnar! Get out of here! A glance over my shoulder told me he'd already taken off, straight toward the closest shore. He was almost out of sight in the trees.

I started across the ice. Jason was out of the SUV, and Molly raced right to him. He put a hand on the firearm on his belt as she approached, but she didn't slow down. She threw herself into his arms.

My eyebrows flew up. She was turning herself in?

I took my time making my way to solid ground, not wanting to fall again. As it was, I'd be one great big bruise tomorrow. I watched Jason put Molly in the back seat of his SUV, then he stood waiting for me. As soon as I was close enough to hear, he called, "Are you okay?"

I nodded. "Fine."

He offered a hand as I climbed up the small embankment into the snowy parking lot. "I heard everything through your phone. Molly's under arrest."

My phone. I pulled it out and looked at the screen. Jason had since hung up, but it showed the call had run for twenty minutes. I slipped it into my pocket, marveling that cell service had worked well enough for him to eavesdrop on us. Maybe it was magic. "How did you find me?"

"I couldn't sleep, so I went to the store to talk to you this morning. Your grandfather told me you were with Molly at Stony Lake. When I called and you answered but weren't there, I got concerned and got in the truck. The signal came in clearer when I was halfway here, and I could hear you were in trouble. I stepped on the gas." He frowned. "But Molly seemed pretty happy I was here. She begged me to arrest her and get her away from the witch and the polar bear under her control."

I blinked a few times, my gaze sliding to the SUV. I couldn't see Molly through the tinted glass, but I imagined her in there, watching us. "The what now?"

Jason guffawed. "I don't know what you did to her, but she's convinced you cast a spell at her, and that a polar bear was out there threatening her at your behest." He laughed harder. "I guess her mind snapped. Probably couldn't handle what she did." He clucked his tongue and shook his head. "Killing her own brother with an ice smashing tool. Unbelievable."

"Yeah. I guess you're right. Her mind snapped." I rubbed my arms.

"You're cold. Get in. I'll drive you home."

"With Molly in there?"

"There's a partition between the front and back seats. You'll be able to see her, but she can't get to you." He reached for me. "You're sure you're okay?"

I rushed into his arms, only slightly less enthusiastically than Molly had. "I am now."

Chapter 18

"Molly confessed to everything. She wants to be moved to a bigger city, and she'll have to be for trial anyway, so I'm taking her in the next couple days." Jason sat across from me the evening after my ordeal with Molly, twirling a teacup between his hands. I was finally getting a chance to try out Charlie's. "She wants to get as far away from Frost Peak as possible."

I put another small scoop of sugar in my tea. "This place must be nothing but bad memories for her now."

He grinned. "She's afraid of you and the imaginary polar bear. Couldn't stop blathering on about it."

I forced myself not to squirm, though I wanted to. I dropped my gaze. The server appeared with our salads, and I smiled in relief at her. Then, I made quick work of drizzling salad dressing on it and taking a big bite. Jason attacked his slower, but the topic of Molly's not-so-insane ramblings was, thankfully, dropped.

The salad was delicious. I hadn't had fresh vegetables in a few days, and all the physical exercise earlier in the day had made me ravenous. I was completely engrossed by my plate but slowly realized Jason was watching me and smiling. "Is there something on my face?"

"No. I just like watching you enjoy yourself."

"Oh." I wiped my lips with a napkin just in case. Then, for good measure, I swiped my chin too. I gave him a smile in return. "Thanks."

He set down his fork and leaned on his forearms. "I got ahold of Mickey. He confirmed that Molly hung her coat in his office on days when she came in and chatted with him before her shift. He was trying to get info from her that might help him pin the murder on someone else. Even though he didn't do it, he knew he'd be a suspect."

I nodded, thinking about the missing button. "Oh! That also explains how Mickey knew Lloyd had been hit over the head. She let it slip without telling him she'd done it."

"Yeah." He leaned back and drizzled dressing on his salad. "Now that the murder investigation is over, things should settle down for you."

I took a sip of tea, then winced. I'd made it way too sweet. Maybe my tastebuds were changing. Next thing you knew, I'd be happy with fish all day every day.

I grabbed the glass of water next to it and washed away the icky taste. "I hope so." But my frown didn't match the words.

"What are you thinking?"

I puffed up my cheeks and released the breath. "About Lloyd. It's so sad to me what his life boiled down to. A house that will be torn down. No one to remember him as anything other than an annoying guy whose own sister killed him. I can't help but feel melancholy about it. Like, when I'm gone, what if I don't leave anything for folks to remember?"

He was quiet for a few minutes, then he said gently, "I've only known you a week, Frankie Banksy, and I can tell you without reservation that you won't end up like Lloyd. You and he are polar opposites. You're kind and bright and optimistic, and everyone whose path you cross will remember all of that."

A lump formed in my throat. I smiled around it and nodded, not trusting myself to say anything. I took another sip of water and enjoyed the wonderful feeling his words had evoked. Then I thought of something else. "I'm worried about the new store Mickey Grimes is opening."

"You think he'll take business from your place?"

I wasn't used to thinking of the store as mine. It wasn't, really; though, now I knew it was being left to me. I could wait forever for that to happen. I'd rather keep my grandfather. "I think he could, yes." I was more worried than that, actually. I was almost positive Grimes' place would leech our business away. "The thing is, it'll be new and different. But also, Grandpa is stubborn about how things are done at Spitzer's. He isn't flexible about trying new things."

"And you want to do all kinds of new things," Jason guessed.

I shrugged and picked at my salad. "I don't see the harm in trying out a few different things, really. But I'm not going to fight with him about it."

He regarded me quietly, pursing his lips.

I took the opportunity to indulge in more greens.

Finally, Jason said, "When I worked my first police job in Anchorage, I had a boss who liked to keep things status quo. Everybody knew it, and no one wanted to upset him—he was a really nice guy and a great boss. Anyway, I noticed the way the evidence was catalogued and accounted for was cumbersome, and it was easy to mess it up and get something wrong. I was afraid something would get missed that could help solve a crime. So I decided to go to my boss and make a suggestion for a change. But my buddies talked me out of it. Said I'd upset him."

I pushed away my empty plate and leaned forward on crossed arms. "What did you do?"

"I didn't make the suggestion. And then one day, I found something miscatalogued while I was studying another case. When I matched it with the right case, I realized it could be solved. I had no choice but to go to the chief then. He was super upset."

I drew in a breath, shocked. "Really?"

"Yep. He was upset I hadn't made my recommendation earlier. He said he'd implement it right away. Then he looked me in the eye and told me if I didn't have enough backbone to walk up to him and tell him he was doing something wrong, there was a problem. I told him it was out of respect for him. And that's when he said something I'll never forget."

"What?"

"That I needed to have enough respect for *myself* to speak up if I saw something to speak up about." He leaned back in the booth and regarded me.

I blew out a breath. "Oof," I said.

"Yep. That's how I felt." He winked. "So since I have respect for myself, I'm going to speak up now."

"About what?"

"About the fact that I like you. I'd like to see you. Regularly. On dates. With or without board games." He held out a hand, palm up. "You up for it?"

I considered his hand for a moment as thoughts twirled through my head like seagulls swirling over a picnic on the beach. I was a witch. One who intended to keep learning about magic and growing in what I could do. What happened out on that lake with Molly showed me I could do it. I could control spells and make things happen. I wanted to do more.

And I couldn't tell Jason about that. I'd have to keep it from him, in fact. The situation with Molly outright telling him had made clear it might be difficult at times. Wouldn't that mean I'd be lying to him? And he'd been lied to by a woman before. It had hurt him. Badly. I didn't want to do the same thing to him.

But as I looked at his adorable face, which was so open and hopeful as he held out his hand, I knew I wasn't going to tell him now. I grabbed his hand and squeezed. "I'm up for it."

He looked so happy I was glad I'd made that choice. I'd just have to keep my two lives separate. Be a witch on my own time and just plain old Frankie Banks on Jason's time. I could do that.

Hopefully.

When I got back to the store after dinner, Ragnar sat by the back door. I rushed forward and wrapped my arms around his neck. He leaned into me, almost toppling me sideways. After a big squeeze, I backed up to look in his face. "Thank you for coming to help me today."

"I only wish I could have gotten there faster. I was occupied when you called and not close by."

"Hey, no sweat. I mean, I figure you have your own life outside of being my familiar. You can't be right around the corner from me all the time."

He hung his head. "It's my job to be nearby." His head jerked back up. "Maybe you could move closer to me."

I squinted, suspicious. "Where do you live?"

"Out on the tundra." He said it so matter-of-factly. Like that was an obvious and normal place to live. Well, it was, for a polar bear.

"I ... don't think I can live on the tundra."

"There's a den?" He said it like a question, then dipped his head again. "Humans are so fragile. But there are dangers out there, I suppose. Crevasses. Other polar bears. You're probably right that Frost Peak is the best place for you. You *have* decided it's the best place for you, right?"

A smile crept onto my face, growing wider as I thought about Ragnar, Grandpa, Aput, Nina, and Jason.

A shuffling noise nearby made me look around and find Timber watching us. Ragnar regarded him. They stared intently at each other, and I got the feeling they were having a conversation. Then Timber scurried away.

"What was that all about?"

He wanted me to know he doesn't share his witch's opinion of me. He'll try to sway George's opinion.

"Wow. That's really nice of him. And, to answer your question, yeah. You guys can't get rid of me now. I'm here to stay."

He chuffed and then stretched his neck to rub a cheek on my arm. *Good, my witch. Good. I'll do my best to stay near enough to keep you out of trouble.*

"That's all a witch can ask of her familiar." I hugged him again.

Chapter 19

"This tastes like sunshine." Nina bit into another strawberry and then scrunched her shoulders as juice dripped down her chin. "How many do we have?"

"We got three cases," Aput answered. "They'll probably be gone before lunch." His tone was mournful.

"At least you snagged these," Grandpa said. "Why don't we set aside a case just for us? With that sugar Frankie ordered, we can make some strawberry shortcake."

"That sounds so amazing." I adjusted my weight on the crate I sat on. We were in the back room of Spitzer's General Store, hanging out. I pulled the top off another strawberry and tossed it to Timber, who snatched it expertly out of the air, then placed it delicately between his tiny front feet and took a mini-bite.

I chuckled. "Such manners. Hey, do we have heavy whipping cream? I could make whipped cream for the shortcake."

Aput nodded. "Eleanor Waters ordered some, so we got a couple extra. It's like liquid gold—so expensive." He got to his feet and headed for the door. "I'd better get us opened up."

Nina craned her neck to make sure he was gone, then turned to me. "I can't believe Molly Dawes tried to kill you."

I popped a small strawberry into my mouth and spoke around it. "If it wasn't for that last magic lesson you gave me in the hangar, I don't think I would have been able to get her off me." I swallowed and then leaned forward. "Molly's pretty big."

"You did great, girl," Grandpa said, shaking his head. "I'm just so thankful it went the way it did." He reached to pick up Timber and settled the fox on his lap.

I narrowed my eyes. "You know, I got Molly off me, but if Jason hadn't gotten there when he did, I still would have been in danger without Ragnar. My familiar was there when I needed him."

A frown pulled down the edges of his mouth, and extra wrinkles appeared on his brow. "I'm not going to say I'm not glad the polar bear was there to help you. But I still don't think he's the right familiar for you. He's just too big and obvious to be skulking around town."

I glanced at Nina, who gave a tiny shrug.

Maybe Grandpa was right. I'd been thinking about moving out of the flat above the store. Perhaps I needed to accelerate that plan. A place on the edge of town or maybe even farther out might put Grandpa more at ease with the idea of Ragnar. I wasn't giving up my familiar, not after everything he'd done for me.

Nina seemed to read my thoughts. She hauled herself off her crate. "Now, just because you managed to make a couple spells go the way you wanted, doesn't mean you're a master witch now. You still need lots of lessons. We can do them at my place if you want—it's small but cozy. My ferret will tell you everything you're doing wrong, so that's not so nice. But if you bring him a treat, he may simmer down."

I rolled my neck, trying to ease the stiffness. As I'd suspected, I was banged up, bruised, and sore from slamming into the ice so much yesterday. "I'll save a couple small strawberries as an offering to your familiar for our first lesson," I promised.

"Ooh, he'll like you more than me after that." She waved and left the room.

I finished stretching my neck, took a deep breath, and then decided to go for it. Jason's story about his police chief echoed in my mind. I needed to respect myself *and* my grandfather. "Grandpa, I want to say something to you, but I want you to know first how much I love you."

The area around his eyes crinkled as he smiled. "I love you too. But that sounds an awful lot like you're about to give me bad news." His smile fell away. "You aren't going to tell me you're leaving, are you?"

"What? No!" I shook my head vigorously, until I remembered how sore it was and clasped a hand to the back of my neck with a wince. "I'm not going anywhere. What I want to say is I understand how uncomfortable it must be for you to have me come in and muck about, trying to make changes to systems that have worked for you for years." I pinned him with a look. "Systems that worked for Grandma."

His gaze dropped to Timber, curled up and snoozing on his lap like a cat. He didn't respond.

I gentled my tone. "But if I'm going to eventually take this place over, like in thirty or forty years when you're gone,"—I grinned—"then I think I need to practice first. You know, while you're here to guide me and help me fix anything I mess up."

He was quiet, continuing to stroke Timber for so long I thought he wasn't going to answer. But finally, he met my gaze, and his eyes held their normal twinkle. I was relieved he didn't seem angry. "It's not easy as a parent or grandparent, you know. You were just a child the last time I blinked. Now, you're a lovely woman who's smart and capable. Smarter than this old man, that's for sure."

I shook my head.

He held up a hand. "It's true. And you're right. I need to loosen up the reins on this place a bit." He looked around, fondness evident in his expression. "I've been stubborn and ridiculous. I didn't want to give up anything that your grandmother had a hand in. Anything she and I built together."

I surged forward, kneeling to clasp his hands around Timber's warm body. "You don't have to give anything up. I only want to expand some things. Tweak them."

"You want to improve things—bring the business into the current age." He chuckled and squeezed my hand. Then he leaned closer.

"You want to make things your own and have them work for you. And I'm ready to let you do that. You deserve it. I'm content changing places with you." He straightened his spine and lifted his chin. "It's time to become the wise, stately consultant. I think I can handle that role nicely. Besides, it means I won't have to try to remember so much, and that suits me fine. I'm tired of remembering everything."

I lurched awkwardly to my feet. "Oof." My tailbone was pretty sore. "Thanks. I'll do my best to make you proud and not mess anything up."

"Oh, you'll mess up plenty. All entrepreneurs do. But you could never make me anything but proud."

Before I could respond, raised voices from the front of the store drew our attention. Grandpa set a drowsy Timber on the floor, and we hurried out. Near the door, a crowd had formed around Carla Swanson. Faces wore concern and shock.

Oh, no. What now?

I gently elbowed my way through the crowd to her. "What's going on?"

"Oh, it's just so scary. There's a dear, sweet polar bear trapped in a crevasse on the tundra. Bruce North—you know, the famous outdoorsman—he's getting his gear together to try to help the poor thing. But the bear is weak. I'm not sure he'll make it." Carla shook her head and tsked. "Bruce said he thinks the bear was here in town and heading back out when he fell in. He spotted the poor thing from his snowmobile while he was heading here from Cross Creek."

Murmurs went up in the crowd, but I couldn't understand their words. All I could think about was what Bruce had said about the bear having been in Frost Peak. There was only one polar bear I knew of that came to town regularly. That had been here last night.

Blood seemed to freeze in my veins as I frantically searched for Nina's face in the crowd. When my eyes met hers, I knew from her expression that she'd figured out the same thing I had. We knew the polar bear stuck in the crevasse. The one near death.

Ragnar.

Also by Amity Allen

Poppy Parker Witch Cozy Mysteries

Poison & Potato Salad

Gunshots & Girlfriends

Needles & Knitters

The Most Murderous Time of the Year Duet

I Saw Mommy Killing Santa Claws

Have Yourself a Deadly Little Christmas

Frost Peak Cozy Witch Mysteries

Polar Opposites

Polar Fleecing

Polar Energy

About the Author

Amity grew up reading every mystery she could get her hands on, burning through everything by Agatha Christie in record time and wanting to be Nancy Drew when she grew up. After writing books in other genres for the past few years, she's finally come home to her true love - cozy mysteries.

Amity and her husband live in L.A. (lower Alabama) with a houseful of teenagers and a half dozen pets. Besides books, Amity's favorite things are football, needlepoint, fried shrimp, and sweet tea.

Sign up for Amity's book club to receive new release updates and sales here: http://eepurl.com/coqgxX

Made in the USA
Middletown, DE
28 November 2023

43864500R00102